A LEAP INTO LOVE

A Sweet Regency Romance Novella

Alina K. Field

For Jim

Can a gentleman be too charming?

The ladies of Upper Upton think so.

And it's almost Leap Day, when a man who refuses a lady's proposal of marriage must offer a forfeit.

When the single ladies of the village conspire to teach their charmer a lesson that might bankrupt him, the town's loveliest young widow steps up to warn him. His secrets and hers make them a perfect match—and she's the lady he wants.

But she won't accept his proposal, not even to rescue him.

As Leap Day approaches, the clock is ticking. Can he convince her in time to say yes to his offer and take a leap into love?

PROLOGUE

London
25 December, 1818

The glowing fog of the short December morning shed a weak light through the dormer windows as Ameline wiped scurf and fluids from the small raging body in front of her. The kicks, the startled, tight breaths, the vacant screams, made her blink back tears. The little one's panic was too much like his mother's, too fresh, too stark. Between Baxter and Mrs. Crawford, they'd managed to bring out the child and the afterbirth. God only knew how.

She forced her fingers to the familiar work, cleaning, comforting, counting fingers and toes, and the moments until the wet nurse arrived.

And then she'd move on to a familiar task, made unfamiliar—cleaning the new mother.

The newly deceased mother. Despite all their efforts, Miss Smith's breathing had just stopped.

Ameline held the baby close and wiped tears with the back of her hand. She'd spent the last frantic moments praying as she hadn't prayed since she'd watched Virgil's sister fade after her last bleeding.

Baxter's two fingers came away from the young woman's neck, and Mrs. Crawford put down the wrist she was pressing. They moved aside and conferred in low, somber tones, while the maid, Aggie, stood pressed to the wall, tears streaming.

Death in childbirth was common enough, but Ameline had never yet lost one of her new mothers. She'd never dealt with this part.

At least the poor babe had survived, yet this little boy would grow up never knowing the woman who'd given him life.

Impulsively, she settled the child onto his mother's chest and his crying paused.

Miss Smith's eyes fluttered and she drew in a sharp breath.

"She's alive," Aggie shouted.

From *The Marquess and the Midwife*,
Chapter 12

CHAPTER ONE

Village of Upper Upton
26 February, 1820

When the Ladies' Society for the Improvement of Village Life gathered, discussions could drag on.

Mrs. Myra Smith stood at a distance, watching the exhalation of so much talk fog the air in the unheated assembly rooms of the Royal George Inn. From her station near the door, she kept an eye on the boy who'd marched off to the far end of the room, away from the ladies.

The Society's grandiose title always made Myra smile. Stuffy-sounding though it might be, the Ladies' Society did have a valuable purpose. Village life could be dull, and didn't she know that well.

It could also be closed-minded, a trap Myra was always dodging. She was here today representing Longview, the nearby children's home that had brought so many interesting characters to Upper Upton—the teachers, ladies of questionable background like herself, and the children, London's outcasts, who'd found shelter, and training, and love.

Longview had been generously endowed by the Lords Cathmore, Hackwell, and Wallenford, much as their lordships had endowed this whole village, trying to make the residents of Longview more palatable to the good citizens of Upper Upton. Even this inn had been thoroughly modernized and expanded. Their lordships had even plucked the handsome innkeeper from among their former military comrades.

Thoughts of the man reminded her, she and Barty should be on their way. "The room is quite adequate to your needs," Myra said. "The children and I shall certainly see to—"

The door to the assembly rooms *whooshed* open, silencing her.

A wide smile flashed her way, and she caught her breath. "Mr. Grant," she said with a clipped curtsy, remembering what she was dealing with.

True to his nature, Alexander Grant turned that handsome gaze on the other three ladies and bowed all around. "Such loveliness brightens the dreary aspects of this day."

His grin widened, and his dark hair sparkled in the light from a tall window. The cold February rain had dampened his coats and breeches and ruddied his cheeks under the dark stubble. Warmth rose in Myra. She shook herself, searching for words.

She need not have bothered.

"A thorough cleaning of these rooms is in order." Miss Eleanor Gurnwood, the new vicar's spinster sister, was nothing if not direct. Myra rather liked her, though she was careful to steer clear of the good woman's questioning. "Did you not have them cleaned after the last Assembly, Mr. Grant?" Miss Gurnwood turned her gaze back to the ladies. "When did the village last assemble here?"

"It was last spring." Miss Charity Putnam moved her round little body closer and peered up at the innkeeper beseechingly.

If she wasn't careful, the girl would turn those charms on the wrong man.

"Was it not, Mr. Grant?" She batted her lashes.

"Charity," the third woman cautioned.

Miss Sally Fitzhugh and Miss Putnam were good friends—and where a marriageable man was concerned, also firm rivals. But while Miss Putnam always had a hop in her step, Miss Fitzhugh tended to sail along at a funereal pace, weighed down by her innate glumness.

Now, Miss Fitzhugh sent Mr. Grant a tremulous smile, a sure sign she was up to no good. "We had smaller gatherings at the church hall. I fear the failure to tidy up here was with us ladies, Miss Gurnwood. And of course, the late vicar's illness and last year Mr. Grant's unfortunate loss—"

"Yes, yes, well," he said, swiping a hand through his curls, scattering droplets.

Drat, but it *was* raining again. She and Barty would have a damp walk home.

His smile turned on Myra and steam rose around her. "If you'll but send me young Barty," he waved a hand at the boy who still stood at the far end of the room, shifting from foot to foot, "and some of your other children, Mrs. Smith, we'll have it all put to rights, and some coin for their labors."

"That is just what we are discussing," Miss Gurnwood said.

"And why Mrs. Smith was, er, gracious enough to take time away from her...employment...and join us," Miss Putnam added.

"Excellent." He beamed again at Myra, and she fought the melting inside her.

Her hands curled into fists. This man was a sure test for a woman like herself, one that she *would* withstand. And dash it all, she must be cordial. For all she knew, he was only a flirt. No one had shared stories of him despoiling women or dallying with maidens, not even after his wife's death the year before. His good looks and charm would pay off soon enough, and he'd find a new wife who would fill his bed and risk death in childbirth for the pleasures there.

She shook off her rattlebrained response to his flummery. It was best to remember the price of flirting that went too far.

"You ladies will be happy to know I've just come from an auction near Crawley. I've some plain worsted you might like for the children, Mrs. Smith, and some very fine muslins and silks that all of you might like. With Lady Cathmore, Lady Hackwell and Lady Wallenford bringing guests to the assembly, our local ladies will want to shine."

Charity Putnam clapped her hands, squealed, and began to chatter.

Myra chewed on her lip. In a few short weeks, the village of Upper Upton would hold an Easter week assembly in these rooms attached to the grandly-named Royal George, the town's only inn. The mourning for the old King George would be ended, as well as Lent, that period of solemn penance. The patronesses of Longview were bringing guests, hoping to inspire more charity.

Whether she herself would attend the assembly to supervise the older children helping there was entirely in question. Yet she would dearly love a new dress, something pretty and stylish. She would dearly love to dance and flirt, perhaps even tease back with the handsome Alexander Grant, as Miss Putnam was doing.

But Miss Putnam had pointed out the truth. Myra was a mere employee of Longview, and grateful for it. There'd be no Easter rising to end her period of penance.

She smoothed a hand over her pelisse and rubbed at a hole in her glove.

"Shall I deliver the worsted, then, Mrs. Smith? I shall give a good price."

Heat shot to her cheeks. "I'm afraid I was woolgathering," she said. "I'll ask the headmistress about it, and we shall send a note."

He bowed all around again and departed.

Miss Putnam grabbed Miss Fitzhugh's hands and hopped a few steps of a jig. "I shall claim a dance with that handsome man."

"He's an inveterate flirt," Miss Fitzhugh said, "as are you, Charity."

"You must have a care," Miss Gurnwood said.

"Over a dance with an eligible widower?" Miss Putnam exclaimed. "Pish-posh. Tell me you would not like to dance with him yourself, Miss Gurnwood."

The vicar's sister smiled, and then laughed, as did Miss Fitzhugh.

Myra forced a chuckle and eyed Barty. The ladies had forgot his presence, and he'd turned his back on them, seeming transfixed by something on the other side of the window.

But Barty was thirteen, and Myra had no doubt he was listening intently.

She cleared her throat and tried to catch Miss Gurnwood's eye.

"He is Scottish gentry, I hear," Miss Fitzhugh said.

"A friend to Lord Cathmore and Lord Hackwell," said Miss Putnam. "And they are patrons of the children's home. What have Lady Cathmore and Lady Hackwell said about Alexander Grant, Mrs. Smith?"

"Naught that I've heard," Myra said. "We do not..."

We do not share tales. The patronesses of Longview never shared tales, their own pasts being also a bit murky.

"Mrs. Smith doesn't gossip," said Miss Gurnwood. "Nor should you, Charity Putnam." She softened the words with a smile. "And we are not alone." She inclined her head toward the boy.

Myra roused herself. "Barty." She beckoned the boy who zigzagged across the dusty floor and came to stand in front of her.

"We've not settled on a plan," Miss Gurnwood said.

Myra swallowed a sigh and patted the boy's shoulder. "Go see to the donkey, the cart, and our packages. I'll be right along."

Barty scooted off with a flap of the door. It didn't close all the way, and she wondered if he was on the other side listening.

"To be sure." Miss Putnam tightened her bonnet strings under her plump chin. "Well Miss Gurnwood and Mrs. Smith neither of you were here last spring, nor did you meet Mrs. Grant. I'm not speaking out of turn to say that never was a woman less inclined to—"

"Charity..." Miss Gurnwood cautioned.

"She was mope-about," Miss Fitzhugh said. "For months on end, we heard. He had to put her old aunt to tend to the boy and often the taproom."

"We were never so surprised as when she turned up with child."

"*Charity*." Miss Gurnwood sighed and shook her head. "But that explains it. I have seen that a persistent malaise in a man or woman can tax a spouse severely. I imagine part of his good nature comes from having the pall lifted and some stability restored to his routine."

"Oh, he's always been jolly."

"A convivial flatterer."

"An eligible, handsome man, in need of a wife and a mother. His boy is a handful, but they say the baby girl is a sweet one," Miss Putnam said.

"If he but manages the inn properly, instead of floating about dabbling into speculative trading in goods, he can hire a nurse to look after the children." Miss Fitzhugh eyed Myra. "One of your older girls would do, Mrs. Smith. What Mr. Grant needs is a nursery maid to manage the children, and a wife who can take a stout hand with the inn staff. And I've always been good at supervising servants."

"If he were to choose you, Sally. But remember, he smiles at *all* of us without pity."

"He does make a lady think he's interested, even some of the older widows."

"And he *needs* a wife. There are so few eligible men in this valley, and none so handsome. It is not fair for him to not marry. We shall have to bring him to heel for one of us."

Miss Fitzhugh's chin shot up, and she snapped her fingers. "Charity. This is a Leap Year."

M iss Putnam's mouth dropped open, and she grasped her friend's hands again. "Leap Year. Leap Day. In..." She counted on her fingers. "Three days' time. You are brilliant, Sally. Mr. Grant *will* have one of us."

"Or his forfeit will be...a pair of gloves."

Miss Putnam shook her head vigorously. "The cloth. And not the worsted either. Let that go to Longview. We'll have the muslin or silk, and proper new gowns for the assembly, or one of us will have *him*."

"He'll be put in his place," Miss Fitzhugh said.

"How?" Miss Gurnwood asked. "What do you mean to do?"

"On Leap Day, a girl may ask a man's hand in marriage," Miss Putnam said, "and if he says no, he must pay a forfeit. Is it not perfect? He, such a flirt, and so in need of a wife, and having a stock of cloth likely too dear for most of us. You must propose to him also, Miss Gurnwood."

Miss Gurnwood's cheeks flamed. Perhaps even the vicar's plain sister was smitten by Mr. Grant's charms. "I will not," the lady said.

Miss Fitzhugh shrugged. "There are others who will. Why even Mrs. Smith might be included. Would you not like a new gown for the assembly?"

Swindle the man out of a gown by proposing marriage? The thought was appalling. The ladies were beastly.

Still, she could not afford to be on the bad side of the ladies of Upper Upton.

Myra made herself smile and stepped toward the door. "I do not wish a new gown," she said. "And I shall not ask Mr. Grant to marry me."

"Would you not ask my brother?" Miss Gurnwood asked. "Such a good wife you would make him, and I fear he will never bring his head out of the spiritual clouds long enough to..."

At Miss Gurnwood's pause, Myra quickly formed her lips into another smile. The lady must have seen the horror racing through her. The vicar was a reserved young man whose sermons put the children to sleep. And Myra also, if she had the courage to be honest.

Myra shook her head. "Your brother is a fine man, but I'll not embarrass the both of us that way. I'll not marry...again."

"Why ever not?" Miss Putnam cried. "You'd have a proper home for you and your babe, the chance for more children."

She swallowed an angry impulse and managed yet another smile. "My son and I do have a proper home and, next door to our cottage, I have a whole houseful of children to care for." She put her hand to the door latch. "And I do thank you for including them in your plans for the assembly. They shall be thrilled to help. Send word to me when you want them to clean. Good day to you."

Alex waved to Barty as he darted past and hefted the bolts of cloth, moving down the corridor to the store room, passing the door to the assembly rooms.

Voices poured through the partially open doorway.

"I do not wish a new gown. I shall not ask Mr. Grant to marry me."

That voice caught him up, and he paused. Myra Smith would not ask him to marry her. What the devil were the women on about?

"Would you not ask my brother? Such a good wife you would make him, and I fear he will never bring his head out of the spiritual clouds long enough to..."

That was the vicar's sister, and her words pricked him. The man of God would try to poach the loveliest widow in the village, her with a fatherless child needing raising? What did a vicar with his head in the spiritual clouds know about raising a boy?

"Your brother is a fine man, but I'll not embarrass the both of us that way. I'll not marry ...again."

He smiled. A wise lass she was. He'd seen her babe, and he was a lively one. The vicar would not make a kindly stepfather to his sort, nor was he the man for the comely Mrs. Smith, and she knew it.

But there'd been hesitation in that last declaration, and wasn't he the man for the challenge?

"You'd have a proper home and children," Miss Putnam said.

"My son and I do have a proper home, and next door, I have a whole houseful of children to care for."

Even better. The lass had shown herself willing to care for other women's children. Perhaps she'd never fret about not birthing any more.

Footsteps approached the door, and he hurried away on stealthy feet, smiling.

On the short walk to Longview, Myra huddled against the dreary dampness, thankful that Barty was silent. And perhaps he would continue so, seeing that he had a dream of employment in Mr. Grant's stable. If the subject came up, she would remind him to hold his tongue on the gossip he'd heard. Until then she would bide with him in silence instead of waking what might be a sleeping dog.

And she couldn't seem to drag her own thoughts back from Alexander Grant.

The man was a charmer, true, and handsome, and a widower and the proprietor of the only inn in the town, and besides that, he was gentry with an education, and a former captain of the army.

But from what Myra could see, he wasn't rich, nor was he putting on airs pretending to be so. The inn, on a side road, had very little custom other than the townsfolk and the patrons when they visited. How he'd put together the coin to buy cloth so dear that day, she didn't know. But she could see, even if Miss Putnam and Miss Fitzhugh could not, it was a kindness for him to bring in good cloth to sell, and good business too.

What the women planned to do was wrong. It was more than a bit like thievery. Surely Miss Gurnwood would not take part in the plot. She must talk to the lady before Leap Day. Or perhaps she could talk to the vicar.

Or...she could warn Mr. Grant. He could go away early on the twenty-ninth and come back late that night.

She hurried up the steps into the grand old manor house that Lord Cathmore had purchased a few years earlier for this home. She'd collect her babe, Arthur, from the nursery, ask Mrs. McClintock about the worsted, and hurry back to the inn to warn Mr. Grant.

CHAPTER THREE

"'Tis a missus you're needing, Alexander."

Alex grinned at the older woman juggling the infant. Olivia Nash was his late wife's great-aunt. She'd attached herself to the family early on, and made the journey down from the north to this Sussex town. And thank God for it.

The wee one's legs paddled like a duck snatched out of the loch. "Crawling everywhere, she is," Auntie Liv said, "faster than my old bones can follow. I'll say again, 'tis a missus you're needing, Alexander."

"Aye, auntie. And these long winter nights have been fierce cold."

Auntie Liv rolled her rheumy eyes at him, making him laugh. He went to her and hoisted the babe who gave him a drooly smile and giggled when he smacked a noisy kiss on her cheek.

His daughter had no clue of the father who'd bred her or the mother who'd birthed her, and that was just as it should be. She was his sacred trust now. He'd raise her just as his own, and find her a mother with gentle ways and sense in her head.

The door slammed open, letting in a sharp blast of chilled air and a flying wool-clad knee-high cannonball.

"Papa," Wills shouted as he always did.

He locked his knees just as the small body slammed into him.

"And my eggs, William?" Auntie Liv raised an eyebrow.

The little boy's mouth dropped open, and he hung his head.

"Well and glad I am you forgot else they'd all be cracked and dripping down onto your father's boots."

Alex rested his palm on the boy's head. Tall for his age, was the boy. He'd be a big man like Alex, like his da. "And how were your lessons today?"

Wills's eyes sparkled. "I'm learning to sum numbers. I can show you."

The village's dame school was better than average, thanks to the patrons of Longview.

But he would need to think soon about a proper school for his boy. An innkeeper didn't have time to tutor, though he himself had enough education to pass on.

"I've an idea, Wills," he said. "Why don't you show me your sums with Auntie Liv's eggs? Bring them back whole and we'll do the counting together."

"And close the door, William," Auntie Liv shouted after the boy.

When the baby began to fuss, Auntie Liv dipped out a bowl of gruel and took her. "And the auction?" she asked.

"Good cloth, fresh off the boat. You'll have a new dress."

She harrumphed. "Ill-got?"

"Not by me. Seized mayhap by the Revenue men, but not stolen. 'Twill make us a pretty penny."

"That and the subscriptions from the spring assembly."

"Aye, well, I've promised the use of the rooms at no cost."

A horn blew outside. Odd, since Longview was so far off the main roads there was seldom demand for a change of teams, and in fact, few horses in their stable.

"Don't frown so. The men will turn up their noses at the ladies' punch and spill into the inn room for their pints. And speaking of that, I'd best take myself to the till and relieve Webster."

"And what of using the eggs for sums?"

"Send Wills out, and we'll work with some pennies instead." He tweaked his daughter's nose and left.

"Is he in?"

The booming voice from the entry hall sent his stomach thudding and slowed his steps.

He shook it off. Best hurry along and face up to this visitor.

Alex found his burly servant pulling at his hair.

The gruff visitor handed off his damp beaver hat, revealing thick dark hair, gone grayer since his last visit.

So there was trouble afoot. "I'll see to the gentleman," Alex said. "Send in a plate of beef and a tankard."

"And two glasses worthy of a proper whisky," the guest said, drawing a bottle from the depths of his pockets.

"Aye. We'll be in the best private dining room, Webster."

Webster's dazed look lifted, and he grinned.

The Royal George had but one private dining room, unless they wanted to move a table to the assembly rooms in back.

"What brings the laird's favorite factor into bluidy England?" Alex asked, taking the older man's overcoat, directing him into a chair near the fire, and moving a table closer. "So soon after the last visit, and in deep winter too. You might have waited until after the lambing. 'Tis a far better journey in late spring."

"'Tis a misery at any time, and you know it."

Alex added a log to the fire and settled into a chair. "Well, MacNab?"

The door opened, and they remained silent while Webster set out a tankard and two glasses. "Food be ready soon," he said, and left.

MacNab gulped ale, wiped his mouth, and poured out two glasses of whisky, handing one to his host. "Slàinte," they both said, saluting and tossing back the shots.

The smooth burn down his throat brought back pleasant memories of a youth gone awry.

And then unpleasant memories slithered in. Alex laughed, shaking them off. "And glad I am you've shortened the time between these bottles, MacNab. And now you've softened me up with good drink, you might as well deliver your blow whate'er it might be."

MacNab rolled his Adam's apple with a great crusty throat-clearing, and Alex gripped the chair arms.

"Old Grant's not dead," MacNab said, "So you can cease strangling the chair." He let out a long breath. "Young Grant is well, also. But the last bairn died. The mother lives, though young Grant wishes she didn't. Has his eye on another lass, he says, a good breeder, he calls her, with a good purse."

Numbness crept up his legs, into his belly. He reached for the bottle and poured a fresh shot before the numbing could reach his arms.

He'd heard the contempt for *young Grant* in the other man's voice, but he was past caring.

"Though your missus faired ill with your last one, old Grant wishes now he'd sanctioned that marriage."

The hair on his neck prickled. "But he didn't."

The bairn be damned, if it's even his. Your brother shall not marry that bit o' muslin, nor shall you. And if you dare to defy me, you can sell your commission and live on it. You'll not get a penny more from me.

"Aye. But he sees now, he'd have had the little lad close, to train him up proper, teach him the running of things if need be. And..." He steepled his hands, tapping his fingers together. "And he might have had you near at hand also."

Old Grant's bloody fool of a younger son.

"He sees that now, Alexander." He bit his lip, frowning.

"It's too late, MacNab. My life is here."

"And the widow you have your eye on—"

The door opened, and Webster appeared, but with no tray in hand, Alex noticed. Of a sudden, a dark head shot past, and Wills barreled into his arms.

Then Wills spotted the old factor and stepped back, eyes wide.

"Old Mr. MacNab is come for a visit again, Wills. Go and shake his hand."

The boy did so, eyes glowing.

"Wills is here to show me the mathematics he learned today," Alex said.

"No, Papa. I mean, yes, but look who has come." He ran to the door and returned with a lady in hand.

Not just any lady, but Mrs. Smith, and she had her young Arthur resting upon her shoulder.

CHAPTER FOUR

Her bonnet had slipped back, freeing a few locks of golden hair, and her cheeks were pink from the cold, though more color flooded them now.

A lovely girl she was, and somehow, on his last visit, MacNab had twigged his interest in her.

She glanced from him to MacNab and back again. "Oh, I do beg your pardon," she said. "William, your father is busy. I will...I will come back...perhaps tomorrow."

"Wait, Mrs. Smith." Alex shot to his feet as he should have done the minute she entered. A poor example he was for his son. "Is aught wrong at the home?"

"No, no, of course not, I...wished to speak to you about...about the worsted." She nodded. "And it will keep until the morrow. Good night."

And she was gone.

MacNab's mouth firmed. "Worsted?"

Sudden anger spiked in him. MacNab had not bothered to rise for the lady, and here he sat, eying Wills.

Neither Old Grant nor MacNab would interfere again between him and a woman. Nor would MacNab snatch his son up and carry him off to either Old or Young Grant.

Alex grabbed the boy by his shoulder. "Get your hat and coat then, we have business to see to. Webster, bring MacNab another tankard and his meal, and then set him up in the best bedchamber."

And he left, snatching up his hat on the way out.

It was almost full night, but he spotted her in the middle of the inn yard where she'd paused to juggle the fretting child. He hurried to catch up.

"Let me take the lad." He extended his arms and the babe, shocked out of his fussing, allowed himself to be lifted away from his mother. The boy screwed up his face, preparing to squawk, but then Wills appeared, distracting him yet again.

"Where are we going, Papa?"

"We're walking Mrs. Smith and Artie home."

"I'm sure that's not necessary," the lady said, reaching for the boy.

He put up his free hand. "And I'm sure it is. It's full dark."

"It's but a short walk, and I know the way well."

"Wills, grab a lantern from the stable, and you'll be our lamp boy."

The boy shot off again.

Arthur squirmed in his swaddling. She'd wrapped him in a heavy quilt.

Barty had accompanied her that afternoon with the donkey cart. She must have gone all the way home before returning to the inn with Arthur.

He lifted a corner of quilt. The babe sported two layers of dresses. He needed some proper warm clothes. "It's cold, lass, and it's dark, and you've got a heavy load here. How old is Arthur now?"

She hesitated, choosing her words. A girl with secrets, as he suspected.

He didn't care. Where women were concerned, he trusted his instincts. He'd known what baggage he'd married before. Mrs. Smith was different.

"Just fourteen months yesterday. He was born Christmas day, year before last."

"He's a big 'un. So was my Wills. Auntie Liv has most of his clothing stored away. She'll be glad to see Artie put them to good use. I'll have her see if there's anything for him, shall I?"

She blinked, looked away, and then heaved a great sigh. "That would be very kind, Mr. Grant." She chewed her lip. "The girls are gaining in skill with the needle. They do well with the swaddling and gowns for the newborns, but I haven't had them take on sewing for this one. He grows so fast, it's difficult to keep up. And fitting this squirming boy! Oh, but the girls are improving apace in their dressmaking. And their embroidery—well. We'll find work for them in the better modiste shops, I'm sure of it."

It was the most words he'd heard from her at one time, and a sign of her nerves. 'Twas a good harbinger of his prospects if he could make such a composed lady so nervous.

Wills ran out of the stable swinging the lantern.

"Easy with that," Alex said. "Hold it steady. You may go ahead of us, son, but you must walk."

The boy grinned and scuttled ahead.

"Walk," Alex called. He glanced at Mrs. Smith and caught his breath. The smile on her face lit up the night.

She genuinely liked children, even the rapscallion Barty who'd accompanied her earlier today. He'd noticed her kindness before, and that smile reaffirmed it. But the warmth he felt now had naught to do with her affection for his boy or her own child.

They stepped out of the inn yard and onto the road. Arthur settled himself on his shoulder and snuffled his neck.

He should offer the lady his arm, but she'd put some distance between them, walking in the other wheel rut. "And so what is the verdict on the worsted?"

She bit her lip. "The worsted." She sighed and squinted at Wills who was ranging far ahead. "We shall buy some of it. Depending upon your price, of course. Mrs. McClintock will be along tomorrow to examine it and talk to you. But in truth..." She stopped, bit down on her lip again and raised her eyes to him. "There is a plot, Mr. Grant. I feel honor-bound to tell you. You must..." Her gaze skittered along the bushes hedging the lane as if someone lurked there eavesdropping. "You must leave town on twenty-nine February. There is a plot."

Twenty-nine February. "A plot."

"Yes."

Twenty-nine February was Leap Day.

The fog lifted. He'd heard of the tradition but never seen it practiced: on Leap Day a lass could propose marriage to a lad. Miss Gurnwood wanted Mrs. Smith to propose to her brother. The stringy young vicar needed a wife. And what had that to do with a plot against himself?

"They mean to conspire, all the unmarried ladies in town. They mean to ask you to marry them."

He swallowed a chuckle. He'd drawn ladies to his handsome self since he'd begun sprouting whiskers. It was good to know he still had the knack. "And why would they do that?"

Her chest rose with a quick breath. "Why? You're a widower, they say, and in need of a mother for your children."

"Is that all?"

She pressed her lips together. "A man who is...well-spoken, reasonably young, and well-established is rare in a village like this."

"And braw and handsome."

"Yes, and a...a...well, I must say it: a man friendly with all the ladies. They mean to take you to task. They mean to ask you to marry them, and when you say no, they mean to ask as a forfeit the silk and muslin cloth you purchased at auction today."

Artie squirmed and looked to his mother, sensing her disquiet.

He patted the plump bottom, and the babe settled. "*If* I say no. And of course I'll have to since I'm not some eastern potentate setting up a harem. It's a diabolical plan. Not too far ahead, Wills," he called.

"So you see, you must leave."

"I'm not one to run from trouble, Mrs. Smith."

Not any kind of trouble. As an officer of the 42nd Foot, he'd fought every skirmish he came across with nary a scratch. It had been an act of charity, taking food to a sick family in Lisbon, that had felled him with a dire case of the mumps and sent him home on half pay.

In the distance Will swung his lantern, well out of earshot.

And Wills was more proof that Alexander Grant didn't run, not even if the problem was not his own.

He'd set his mind to what was right, so he might as well go ahead with it, and directly too. She'd not go away thinking he was anything but dead serious.

He touched her arm.

"Mrs. Smith, there is another way to thwart them."

CHAPTER FIVE

Even in the dark, Myra could feel the intensity of his gaze. Apprehension stirred in her. She was on a dark road with a handsome man.

But he wouldn't accost her with Arthur in his arms and his own boy so nearby.

And, oh dear—this wasn't fear she was feeling, but excitement. Her pelisse was thin, and he hadn't stopped to don gloves, and warmth spread from where his strong hand touched her arm.

There was nothing to fear from him but a great deal to fear from herself. She shook off his arm.

"What other way is there, Mr. Grant?"

Arthur's snuffling breaths signaled that he'd fallen asleep. Mr. Grant smoothed a palm over her boy's back and took in a deep breath.

One might think he was nervous, this man who chattered so easily with everyone, even herself.

"If they ask, and I say no, they'll claim a forfeit. But what if I'm already claimed, Mrs. Smith? What are the rules on this? Surely they won't propose to a man who's already betrothed?"

Her chest tightened. He reached for her again and slipped an arm around her shoulder, making her shiver.

"I've watched you with the children, Mrs. Smith."

She snorted. "When could you possibly—"

"At church. Today with Barty. When I've stopped at the children's home. When you've brought the older boys around to do chores. When you've dropped by the inn to visit with their ladyships and their own wee ones. I see when a woman is dissembling, and you are not. You're firm with them, and kind. Wills likes you, and I...I admire you greatly."

"You admire everyone greatly."

A chuckle rumbled up in him. "I'm a rambling fool, my father used to say. 'Tis why your quiet dignity so impresses me."

She shook her head vigorously and choked, trying to find breath.

"Will you marry—"

"*No.*"

William's lantern swung round, and she clamped a hand over her mouth and took a breath.

"All is well, William," she called. "Your father just asked me if, er—"

"I wanted to know if little Artie likes turnip mash."

The boy laughed and turned back on the path.

"Would you not even consider it to save me?"

She heard the humor in his voice. He was playing with her.

As Arthur's father had done.

"You are teasing me Mr. Grant, as you tease every young woman in the village."

"Besides my late wife, I've asked no other woman to marry me. I was quite serious."

"And any one of them would happily say yes to your proposal."

"But not you. You have no interest in marriage."

"I shall never marry again."

"And what of romance?"

She stumbled, and his hand steadied her, sending warmth through her. "Why, you—"

"I see that I've been too direct. I ought to have wooed you first, but the peril from the other ladies—"

"And who would be able to distinguish your wooing from your regular *rambling*? You speak so, so, warmly to everyone."

"I'm not a rake, Mrs. Smith, nor a fribble, nor some popinjay fussing with his neck cloth every minute. Have you heard ill of me in any of those ways?"

"No, but I am new to these parts."

"And I've been here a few years, plenty of time to stir up talk."

She spotted the lights of Longview and the lane that led to her small cottage in back. William knew the way and turned down the lane.

Mr. Grant would take her all the way to her doorstep, and the thought sent a thrill through her.

And then set off alarm bells.

But no, William's presence and Arthur's would protect her.

William reached the door before them and waited.

"'Twill be devilish cold tonight, Wills. Go in and poke the fire and check there's enough wood."

"He's so little. I'm sure I can—"

"*Shhh*. Take this one." He passed a dozing Arthur to her. "I'll send some warm things over for him. Now I've been properly warned, I know what I must do."

He leaned in and pressed his lips to hers, the gentle kiss leaving her breathless.

"Oh," she said when he pulled back.

William appeared in the door, lifting his lamp higher to peer at them. "There's plenty of wood, Papa," he said proudly. "I've poked at the embers, and the fire's coming back."

"Aye," Mr. Grant whispered, unsmiling. "So have I. And I'll raise the flames higher the next time."

And then he and his boy and the lantern were gone.

*****

On Monday morning, Alex stood wiping the counter while Webster moved stools and mopped the dirty floor. The winter night had drawn in a few more of the locals seeking the ready warmth of the inn's hearth.

The headmistress of Longview, Mrs. McClintock, arrived at the same time that MacNab came downstairs. The mule-headed man refused to take meals in his room. He would insist on always being underfoot.

The man's eyes lit when his gaze landed on Mrs. McClintock. A plainly and modestly dressed woman of middle years, she was nevertheless handsome, and possessed of a figure that still turned heads. Where Lady Hackwell had found her, he thought it best not to ask.

"Good day, Madame," MacNab said, bowing.

Alex was having none of that.

"Show Mr. MacNab to the dining room, Webster," he called, "and see to his breakfast."

She curtsied and said with her usual dignity, "I'm here about the worsted, Mr. Grant."

He came round the counter and took Mrs. McClintock's elbow. "We may talk more privately in my quarters." Except for the presence of Auntie Liv and the baby. But he reckoned the lady would not mind the child, and he was counting on both ladies assisting with his plan.

MacNab caught up with him later in the inn yard where Alex was loading a cart.

"Skipped breakfast, did you?" Alex said. The old factor had gone out riding instead, and now he dismounted, looking around for a groom.

"You'll have to use your own man," Alex said. "Mine has gone off on an errand."

"I don't have a man. I rented a chaise, and it's gone back."

"Tie him up, and I'll see to him in a bit."

MacNab edged closer. "What's that you're loading?"

He'd rewrapped the frames of cloth in brown paper. It was cold as a witch's tit, yet a fair enough day and a short enough trip that they should arrive dry and unharmed.

"The worsted."

MacNab let out a laugh. "I did think for a bit it was some code between you and the widow."

"It's real cloth. Here, have a look." He peeled back the brown paper to reveal cloth the same shade as the paper. "Now, tie up that horse or go see to him yourself."

"I can see I didn't backhand you enough when you were a lad. But I'm here to help you now."

Alex paused at the serious tone and studied the other man. "William is my son. He stays here with me."

"And your heart is set upon a widow who lives in a children's home run by a woman who at some point was on the stage—or worse."

Anger flared in him. The patrons of Longview had put out the story that their headmistress was a sea captain's widow, and maybe that was the truth. They'd used the same story for Myra Smith, widow of a seafaring man, they'd said. "You'd best bite your tongue old man. Mrs. McClintock was hired by a countess, and *her* lord would not take kindly to you maligning her."

"Hackwell's lady?"

"Yes."

"And of her, I've heard tales—"

"Say more, and Hackwell will skewer you tongue-first. And I'll hold you down while he does it."

"I've been in London. Mayhap I have some facts to share with you."

CHAPTER SIX

"**A**nd mayhap I don't want to listen to town gossip."

"You're a mule-head yourself, Alex. If you'd listened you might've been spared the trouble of William's mother—"

"Wills is a Grant." He fisted his hand, having just stopped short of grabbing the old man's throat. "What I did, I did for him, not her."

"And Mrs. Smith's babe is not a Grant. I hear tell he's not a Smith, neither. There is no Smith, or rather, there be too many for us to track the one down."

He shrugged, his insides burning. He knew some of her story, and he'd suspected as much. How dare the old man pry into her business?

"You'll want bairns of your own, besides that wee lass in there. And I hear tell, the lady you have your heart set on died when her boy was born."

His head jerked up. "What fool said that? She's very much alive." He thought of their kiss two nights before. "Very, very much."

"'Twas a miracle. Sounds like poppycock to me, but I talked to one of the servants at the home where she delivered. She swears the girl's breath stopped and all. Started up again when the midwife laid the babe upon her." MacNab moved closer. "You'll not want to lose another wife in childbirth."

His insides were dancing, but he moved in on the old man and glared, as was expected. "I'll take my chances."

No chances, that's what he had. Miss Smith would never get with child by him. And now he knew why she never wanted to marry again. Fear of death was a powerful thing.

"What are you about, MacNab?" Auntie Liv's voice rang out across the courtyard. "Doonna be bothering my boy," she said, with a wink to Alex.

MacNab backed away, transfixed by the lady accompanying Auntie Liv.

"Have you everything loaded?" Mrs. McClintock asked as they reached the cart. She glanced up at the clouds sailing along in the breeze. "Still a fine day, but we'd better be off."

"Webster is with the babe," Auntie Liv said. "Best go rescue them both."

He helped both ladies onto the seat.

Mrs. McClintock beamed down at him. "It's good doing business with an honorable man."

"It's all for the children," he said with a wink.

Auntie Liv rolled her eyes. "Well, get back on your horse, MacNab. You've been wanting to take your curious self to Longview, and that's where we're heading."

MacNab hastened to mount and flashed a keen smile at Mrs. McClintock.

Alex dusted his hands and went back to see to his daughter. He had no worries where MacNab and the women were concerned. Either lady could skewer the old man more brutally than any insulted earl.

Myra cooed to the infant as she changed him and handed him off to his mother's breast. The baby's plaintive whines soon ended.

"He's latched on well, hasn't he?"

The young woman laughed. "I've had plenty of practice then, haven't I?"

Myra helped a toddler onto the bed next to her mother and called a girl of about ten over. "You've got your da's meal ready?"

The girl nodded, and Myra patted her cheek. "I'll be off then. Send word if you need me."

"You done as good as Mrs. Dawes," the young mother said. "Might be calling you milady soon also, if a handsome lord wonders through the village."

She laughed. Mrs. Dawes, who had once worked at Longview and served as the village midwife, was now Lady Wallenford. "Not a chance. And the midwife delivered your babe, not I."

"Is it true? Well, I was yelling so loud, an' my eyes squeezed shut, I didn't know."

She laughed again and slipped out the door of the cottage. The dwelling was smaller than her own and housed two adults and now three children.

She must count her blessings.

She'd been called early the day before, just as she was getting the children ready for church. The baby was coming quickly, and the midwife was delayed at another birthing.

Thank the Lord the midwife appeared in time. Myra Smith would never make a midwife. She could help with the walking, with the fetching and boiling, and the cleanup, but she'd never be any good at a rough birth. Mrs. Crawford, the midwife who with Lady Wallenford had delivered Arthur, had tried to train her, but in fact, she'd come near to fainting more than once.

When she reached Longview there were three horses in the drive, two of them attached to an empty wagon painted with the colors of the Royal George. Barty and a couple of the other boys stood around patting the animals and seeing to them, though it was perfectly clear they could leave the animals unattended and go back to their studies.

Though their studies wouldn't help them get jobs as grooms, and that was Barty's aim.

"Be mindful of their mouths and those feet," she called. Mr. Grant's horses seemed to be placid beasts, but horses could be unpredictable. Once as a girl, her pony nearly...

She took a deep breath. That was long ago.

Two of the boys stepped back from the horses, but Barty saluted.

She smiled and went in.

One of the smaller girls held the door while another one struggled with a tea tray. "There's a gent in the parlor with Auntie Liv and Mrs. McClintock," she whispered.

Being staff had its advantages. She could happily dodge that visitor, whoever he may be. "Where's my Arthur?" she asked.

"In the nursery, just down for a nap. Nan has him in hand with the others."

She would have time for a cup of tea and a bite in the kitchen. Then she would check on the interrupted lessons and fetch Arthur when he started wailing.

As soon as she'd sat down to her tea and buttered bread, Auntie Liv pushed through the kitchen door.

"And here you are, my girl." The old lady smiled, her eyes merry. "Is there enough for two?"

She seated Auntie Liv and fetched a clean cup.

"You didn't join us in the parlor," Auntie Liv said.

"I don't like to interrupt. Mrs. McClintock often receives potential donors, and she's better served if I keep the children in hand while they're here."

The lady looked around at the empty kitchen. "And where are they now? Where's the cook?"

She laughed and looked around. Quiet like this usually didn't bode well. "Cook is...I don't know where. She disappears sometimes in the early afternoon for a nap." Occasionally a nip, but no one could fault her given the usual chaos around her. "The older boys are out with the horses. The girls are, I hope, in the conservatory working on their embroidery." She set down her cup. "And you're right, I should see to them."

Auntie Liv's clawed hand came down upon hers. "Hold there. 'Twas unfair of me to ask. One of your teachers is in with them. The nursery maid has the youngest ones in hand, including yours. And I need an escort home."

"I can send one of the boys."

"No. Your boys, I'm sorry to tell you, are filthy."

She'd noticed the mud on Barty's trousers. She hadn't looked closely at the others.

"They found the only patch of mud in all this ice. One fell and dragged the others with him. Mrs. McClintock ordered some of them inside to change and wash."

"Very well." She reached for her pelisse and shawl. "I shall just tell Mrs. McClintock—"

"No, do not interrupt her, else that fool man will want to follow us back to the inn."

"He's a guest?"

"Yes. He's Old Mr. Grant's overseer. Thinks he's laird of the manor himself. Now, I'm all bundled up already and warmed from the tea. You pull on your warm things and we'll go." The old lady stood and helped Myra into the sleeves of her pelisse. "You'll drive."

"Me?"

"Yes. I'm weary. And those beasts will be ill-tempered standing in the cold and being pawed over by all those beastly boys." A grin split her face, and she laughed.

Whatever was afoot in the parlor continued unabated as they tromped past, Auntie Liv gabbing loudly while hanging on to Myra's arm.

Barty handed off the visitor's mount and helped both ladies up and made as if to jump into the empty cargo box.

"You and your muddy self are not coming," Auntie Liv said.

"Barty," Myra reached down and touched his shoulder. "It's very cold for that gentleman's mount. That horse needs to be walked back and forth in the lane. Can you see to it, please? I don't think the younger boys are strong enough."

Indeed, the gelding was nodding his head. Barty hurried back to his charge.

Myra flicked the reins, and the wagon pulled out.

Auntie Liv sent her a sideways look. "Some boys do better with a smack than kind words."

"Some do, for some circumstances, but not Barty, and not on this occasion."

The older lady harrumphed. "You sound like my nephew. Not a grand believer in the switch. Had it applied to his own backside too often, he says."

Myra's heart lifted. Her observations about Mr. Grant had been, so far, correct.

"He's a kind man under all that flummery," Auntie Liv said. "He took me in, he did, without question. Without knowing how much he needed me."

Myra hit an icy patch, and the wagon shifted. She slowed the horses, holding her breath for the old lady's next shared secret.

CHAPTER SEVEN

"When he and my niece—my grand-niece, actually—married, I went along on the honeymoon. And never left. He was kind to her, though she didn't deserve it, and she didn't repay it. Oh, she shared his bed when she was in her good times, but when her mood was dark, there was no consoling her. Alexander never laid a hand to her. Never spoke a harsh word to her, except once when she went after William."

Wills's mother had been a dark-haired beauty, the ladies had whispered. Married to a handsome and charming man, with a beautiful child, and a home. And yet, she was so unhappy. "Was it...was it a love match?" She gave her head a quick shake. "Oh, I beg pardon. That is none of my business. Only one wonders why..."

"Why he married such a miserable girl?"

"As I said. It's none of my business."

"She wasn't always miserable. She was always too pretty for her own good, and, aye, she was head over ears in love."

Myra held her breath. Alexander's wife had loved him, and it had gone terribly wrong. As it might have had Arthur's father married Myra. Love matches didn't always endure.

And of course, in spite of his early declarations, Arthur's father had not loved her after all. When she'd fallen with child, he'd hinted it, then he'd said it outright, and in the end he'd proved it in the worst way possible.

"She was head over ears in love with Alexander's older brother, and when he got her with child, the old man refused to allow a wedding."

Myra's chest tightened. "Wills—"

"Is not Alexander's. He will never tell anyone that, and somehow, I think you will keep his secret."

"Of course."

She would. Unspoken was the fact that Myra had secrets of her own. Everyone believed she was a young seaman's widow, an orphan with no family or friends. Well, and that much was true now.

"So why did he marry her?"

Auntie Liv sighed. "You can imagine that Alexander had more girls chasing him than anyone could count, and some with sizeable dowries. My niece had very little but her respectability, and that she tossed away for a charmer."

"Alexander, er, Mr. Grant, is a charmer."

"Alexander has a conscience. Alexander has honor. That's why he convinced her to marry him, for the sake of the babe. William is a Grant, and may well inherit the laird's grand estate if his scapegrace of a father can't get a child on his wife that will live. Alexander was thinking of William and the future of the Grants."

A shiver went through her. Mr. Grant was a wealthy laird's younger son. "I suppose he moved away because of the...connection."

"He was cast out. Forbidden to marry the girl. He did so anyway. Sold his commission, took the money, and came south to find a position. Eventually...oh, it was after Waterloo...he found his home here. And good thing, as his father cut him off." She grumbled. "Though he sends that interfering man down often enough to spy on Alexander. He means to steal away with the boy, I believe."

"Wills?"

She nodded. "Alexander shared with me the ladies' Leap Day plot. Sunk all his ready coin into that enterprise of the cloth, and I do worry they will snatch it from him."

"Let's talk to the vicar." She had meant to talk to the vicar after services the day before, but she'd been off helping the midwife.

"That pious fool? Much help he'll be. The ladies must be stopped."

The skin on Myra's neck rippled. Auntie Liv had looked away, not meeting her gaze. What was the old lady up to? Surely Mr. Grant had deeper resources than what it had cost to purchase some bolts of cloth.

Though...good silk and fine muslin were far too costly for her, and probably many of the other ladies of the village. So perhaps he had speculated too dearly.

When they pulled into the inn yard, the old groom rushed out to hand them down.

"You'll come in and warm up," Auntie Liv said. "Some hot tea, I think."

She followed reluctantly. Hot tea was welcome, but the handsome man who would likely be serving would make her insides shiver more.

Alex refrained from rubbing his hands together when Auntie Liv appeared leading Mrs. Smith into their private living quarters. The innkeeper's set of rooms was on ground level, with easy access to quell trouble in the tap room. Though when Wills's mother lived, he'd spent many a night on a cot in this sitting room, where he could be close if his boy got up in the night.

Aye, and where he could know when Wills's mother was wandering. He shoved back the unhappy thought and plopped the babe into her cradle, which she promptly tried to scramble out of.

Mrs. Smith grabbed his girl and hoisted her up. "You're an impatient scamp, aren't you? Your Auntie Liv and I would like to shed our coats before you wander about."

Auntie Liv, tied up in her sleeves from Alex's helping, smacked his arm. "You're twisting me up more, boy."

He took his daughter under one arm like a loaf of bread, and did what he could to help Mrs. Smith out of her pelisse.

The lady's cheeks were pink, her nose red as a button. He settled her on one side of the fire and Auntie Liv on the other with the babe, and went for the teapot.

He'd just set the pot down when Webster called for him and Auntie Liv. The cook needed her, and the groom needed Alex.

Mrs. Smith stood to put on her wraps.

"Here." Auntie Liv shoved the babe into her arms. "I'll be right back."

Alex had her alone. The groom's business could wait.

"Where is Wills?" she asked.

"Doing chores. He'll pop along in here just as things get interesting."

She laid a level gaze upon him. "Things will not get interesting between us, Mr. Grant."

Aye, but her cheeks had gone pinker.

A rap at the door brought Webster again. His gaze darted between him and the lady. He shuffled from foot to foot and began to stutter.

"What is it now, Webster?" 'Twas bad to interrupt a master two times in a row when he was wooing.

"Beggin' your pardon, but the groom says to come quick, that it's the boy. He's...fallen...or some such and hurt hisself."

He reached for his hat, and Mrs. Smith jumped up. "I'm coming also." Her gaze darted around the room and landed on a heavy shawl.

When she reached for it, he stopped her. "The babe has had a wee cough. Stay here until Auntie Liv returns. I'll bring Wills along or send for you."

Myra's nerves itched with worry. She tried to avoid thinking the worst—God knew the Longview children were always scraping knees and elbows, but they'd had no serious injuries, and they'd not lost a one of them, not even to illness. Good food, warm beds, and plenty of fresh air kept them healthy. But their clumsiness...

She hoisted the babe and began to pace. When she reached the corner of the room and turned, a tall, older man stood in the doorway.

CHAPTER EIGHT

Well-dressed, and handsome he was, and his gaze raked over her. She edged closer to the fireplace with its many tools.

"You have the wrong room, sir. I'll thank you to leave."

"This is the innkeeper's sitting room, is it not?" he asked, and she heard the thick burr, far thicker than Alexander's lilting tones.

This was Alexander's father's man, sent to keep watch on him. "I'll just go and get Auntie Liv, and you may be seated."

He was not likely to rob Alexander, was he? And Wills was not here to be stolen either.

But the man blocked the door and wouldn't budge.

"You are Mrs. Smith, I believe. I'm MacNab, Grant's man of business. It's you I'm wanting a moment with."

Panic flared in her, and with it, anger. "You are impertinent to barge in like this. You'll move yourself away from that door and let me and this babe pass, or I'll..." She took a deep breath. "There's a boy out there, injured, and in need of my help."

His eyes widened, and his lips quirked. "The boy's all right. I needed to meet you without those two being present."

"And I suppose all is well in the kitchen, also?"

"Aye, other than that woman doesn't know how to properly cook a beefsteak." He smiled and swept out his hand. "Please sit down. They'll be but a few moments discovering the sham."

God save her, he was another charmer.

She sat near the fire and its solid poker and snuggled the babe, whose eyelids were drifting down.

Guilt nagged at her—her own little boy was awaiting her. Yet Arthur was well-cared for, of that she was certain.

MacNab took the chair across from her.

"Where do you hale from, Miss Smith?"

Oh no. Oh no, he wouldn't. He was not going to slip in sly innuendo and poke her for answers. She lived in Upper Upton. It was her home, and he was not going to destroy her standing with the villagers here.

"It is *Mrs*. Smith, and I am an Englishwoman. You are Scottish, I believe? Where, pray tell, is your master Mr. Grant's estate?"

"*Laird* Grant's estate is in...Scotland."

She eased in a breath and prayed for patience. He was matching her evasiveness and trying to impress her with titles. But she knew her DeBrett's. A laird was no more than a rich squire with a great estate.

Flummery. These Scotsmen were filled with it.

"What is it you truly want from me, Mr. MacNab? Best ask quickly. Mr. Grant is no fool, nor is Auntie Liv. They'll return soon."

"Aye. They'll rush back to save you. I want to know the truth. Have you agreed to marry Alexander?"

"*What?*"

"'Tis my mission to learn the truth. I've poked about in your history, and you'll not meet the old laird's standards, I fear, though you're well-spoken enough and appear to have a backbone."

She gazed down at the sleeping babe in her arms and bit back a smile. She was reminded of a scene in a novel she'd read and reread years ago. Pity she hadn't learned the lessons of that story.

"Well?" he asked. "Tell me, girl. Oh, I see the grin you're hiding. You're going to say yes to my nephew." He rubbed his chin. "Laird Grant won't like it."

She shook her head and chuckled. "I was thinking that I feel very much like Elizabeth Bennet."

"Who?"

"A character. In a novel called *Pride and Prejudice*. Her suitor's dragon of an aunt travels to her home to find out if she's engaged to her nephew."

"And is she?"

"No."

He rubbed his chin some more. "But she winds up marrying him."

"Yes. But I'm not Elizabeth Bennet, Mr. MacNab. I'm *Mrs.* Myra Smith." She stood and placed the sleeping babe in her cradle, tucking a shawl around her, sensing him watching her every move.

"I've heard of this plan to swindle young Alex tomorrow," he said. "Don't like it. Don't like it a bit. Foolhardy speculation. I've told both the boys, and I thought Alex at least had listened. Commodities are fine, trade is good, but don't put all your eggs in one basket. The laird will want a high price for helping him."

Her hand went to her heart. *Wills.*

She eased in a breath and tried to speak calmly. "You'll have money put aside, Mr. MacNab. You'll help him."

He rubbed his chin. "You'll ask a Scotsman to throw good money after bad?"

Before she could speak, the door burst open, and Alexander led Wills in by the shoulder. Myra bent to hug the boy.

"You're all right?" she asked.

He nodded, eyes wide, glancing from Mr. MacNab to his father, who glowered with a look she'd never seen on his face.

"Off to bed, Wills." His tone was kindly, the hand that tousled Wills's hair gentle. He grabbed Myra's pelisse, helped her into it, plopped her bonnet upon her head, and took another shawl from a chair back and wrapped it around her. "You and I will talk later, MacNab." He took Myra's arm. "Come, Mrs. Smith, I'll see you home."

She glanced at the door Wills had just slipped through. "But the boy—we should wait for your aunt."

"I'm here now." Auntie Liv plowed through the door, carrying a tray of dishes piled with food and set it upon the table. Her hands went to her ample hips and she glared at MacNab. "You might as well pull that chair over and eat with me. Go on, Mrs. Smith. See to your boy."

Alex reached for the lantern he'd left in the entry and tucked her hand over his arm. "It's a cold night. Are you up to a brisk pace?"

"I am."

"And how was the wee one born yesterday?"

"In good health, mother and child."

"Boy or girl?"

"A boy. Her man was quite happy. He brought in a goodly supply of fuel. They'll not be cold."

When a shiver went through her, he freed his arm and tucked it around her shoulder. "I could feel that I'm in the Highlands, it's been that wintry."

He sensed her tension easing, and smiled. Discussing the weather could put anyone into a snooze, but it would serve his purpose to have the lady relax and warm up a bit.

"The villagers say they rarely get so much snow as we had in January. Was your home in the Highlands, Mr. Grant?"

"I'm afraid so. Far north enough to know this kind of weather well." Now to get down to business. "Is your heart set on midwifery?" he asked.

"Heavens, no. I don't mind helping, but I have a tendency to faint." She paused for a breath. "Arthur's birth was...was not easy. I fear losing a mother." She glanced up at him, and he caught the blue shimmer of her eyes in the lamplight.

God help him, he wanted to kiss her now, here, in the middle of the frozen lane.

"I'm sorry to bring up a painful subject," she said.

"Wills's mother didn't die birthing my little girl. Oh, I know everyone thinks that, but she would have been right as rain if..." He took a breath. "She got up from her lying in and left. She came back days later, bedraggled and ill, starving. She'd caught a fever that settled in her chest."

"Oh. Was it...was she..."

"Mad? No." He pulled her a bit tighter to him. They had indeed kept to a good pace, and the lights of Longview gleamed nearer.

"Everyone thought I went out seeking a doctor, but I followed her to her destination, and she wouldn't come home with me."

"But why?" She shook her head. "No, it's not my business."

"Thank you. I don't wish to speak ill of my children's mother. Now tell me, what did old MacNab say to you?"

"He wanted to question me."

"I shall thrash him for his rudeness."

"No. There is no need. I told him quite plainly what I think of him. And it was a dreadful trick to play on you, telling you your child was injured."

"That's MacNab. It was the only way I would have left you."

They'd reached the front steps, and he pushed open the door. Small heads poked out of the schoolroom, and he heard a long wail. "Artie needs you, I suppose." He waved the children back into their chamber and tugged her close. "But first I must claim one boon from you."

And then he kissed her.

CHAPTER NINE

The caterwauling stopped, and a whispering began, and he didn't care. Mrs. Smith showed she knew a bit about kissing. A true boon it was. Grateful he was. A handful of a woman and sensible and with a mouth made for kissing and—

A throat cleared loudly. He pulled his head away from the lady's and nodded at the handsome headmistress before turning back to his lady.

"Tomorrow is Leap Day," he said.

She clutched at his shoulders. "You must leave town. Go away for the day and come back on the Wednesday."

"Travel on these frozen roads? I have one good mount, and the old man has claimed him."

"We can hide you." She glanced at the headmistress. "Can we not, Mrs. McClintock?"

"You shared the plot with the headmistress? Will *you* also be proposing, madam?"

The headmistress laughed. "Perhaps I shall ask your Mr. MacNab. He spent most of the afternoon in my parlor. I think he is smitten."

"You must hide or go away," Mrs. Smith cried. "We'll not let MacNab take William."

"Grants do not run, nor do we hide."

"Then say goodnight to your lady and take care you don't fall on that ice, Mr. Grant." Mrs. McClintock returned to the schoolroom and shut the door firmly.

He'd been given a chance at another kiss, and he took it.

The message arrived at Longview the next morning. The Ladies' Society would convene at noon to clean and wax the assembly room floors. The older children were requested, and would be rewarded for their service with hot cocoa.

Mrs. McClintock read the note aloud to Myra and then went about gathering children and cleaning supplies.

And Myra fell into a panic.

This had naught to do with her. Except that it did. Mr. Grant had made his intentions even clearer with his second kiss, one that Mrs. McClintock interrupted by carrying Arthur over and handing him to her.

Then the man had insisted on escorting her to her cottage and insuring the fire was stoked, the firewood plentiful. Perhaps she should have slept with Arthur in one of the Longview nursery beds. She'd huddled under heavy covers with her boy, tossing and turning and never truly getting warm.

A woman with a man like Mr. Grant in her bed would never be cold.

She shook off the foolish thought and went to gather her things and make arrangements with Nan for Arthur.

On the walk to the inn, she stopped two snowball fights and rescued buckets and mops from clumsy hands.

"I want to attend an assembly someday," the oldest girl said.

"You'll be serving the punch and sewing up ladies' skirts," Barty said.

The girl stomped her foot. "I want to *dance*. Have you ever danced at an assembly, Mrs. Smith?"

"Yes. I have."

"Was it magical?"

It had been, for a while, for months actually. Until her day of reckoning had come.

"Mrs. Smith?"

"Assemblies and balls can be quite fun, or quite boring," she said. "It all depends on the company." There. That was equivocal enough.

"Did you meet your husband at an assembly?"

She made a mental note to talk to Mrs. McClintock about this twelve-year-old. The girl might dream of fairy tale princes, but one was not likely to show up.

Still, she couldn't put a pall on a child's dreams.

"I did dance with him," she said.

"Will you dance with Mr. Grant?"

"Mr. Grant will be drawing pints for all the men," Barty said smugly. "He'll be like us—working, not dancing."

"That's right. You girls and I will be passing out refreshments, and the older boys will be tending to horses and carriages. Now, let's hurry before the ladies come, and show them what good workers we are. Perhaps the vicar's sister will give you a reference."

But when they reached the inn yard, dismay swept through her. Several carts and a carriage sat parked there.

Her hands curled into fists, and she grabbed for a bundle of mops and led the way across the inn threshold.

"Where is Mr. Grant?" she asked his man of all work, Webster.

"Everyone's so early. Just got the fireplaces started. Best leave your coats on."

"Webster. Where is he?"

"He's just gone in."

She charged through the tap room down the short hallway and into the cavernous room. Mr. Grant saw her and smiled.

"Must I?" he said with a twinkle.

Miss Putnam rested her plump hands on her equally plump hips and smiled smugly. "Yes you must."

"Yes you must," Miss Fitzhugh said. "It's the rule."

Myra looked around at the sea of greedy faces, and anger bubbled over. Miss Putnam and Miss Fitzhugh must have sent the news far and wide that Alexander Grant would part with good cloth today or say yes to taking a wife. Some of the ladies she'd never seen before.

Miss Gurnwood stood between Miss Putnam and Mr. Grant. "My dears—"

"It's the rule," Miss Putnam said. "I asked the vicar, and he affirmed it with a lengthy discourse on the folk customs of England. You must say yes, to one of us, or else everyone you decline will receive a forfeit. I would like to see the cloth and make my choice."

Myra stepped forward. The children crowded behind her. "Children," she said, employing her teacher's voice, "what is the Tenth Commandment?"

Barty, of all of them, poked through the group and fumbled his hat off. "Thou shalt not covet thy neighbor's house, thou shalt not covet thy neighbor's wife, nor his manservant, nor his maidservant, nor his ox, nor his ass, nor any thing that is thy neighbor's."

"Oh well done," Miss Gurnwood cried.

They'd worked extra hard with Barty, who'd once been part of a burglary ring.

"Pish posh," Miss Putnam said. "He may marry me if he doesn't wish to observe the custom."

"And if he accepts you? Will the rest of you swindle him also?" Myra asked.

"We didn't ask Vicar about that," Miss Fitzhugh said. "We assume he does not want any of us."

Miss Gurnwood's shoulders went back. "My brother would say that an affianced man has no standing to make or consider another offer of marriage."

Dear God, please forgive me. Myra lifted her chin. "Then he has no standing, because he has asked me to be his wife, and I have accepted."

CHAPTER TEN

A lex's heart all but burst. He threw his cap in the air and whooped, dancing Myra around in a hasty jig. Her bonnet slipped to the side, and golden locks fell over her cheeks. And she smiled.

But it was a smile laced with panic. If he knew women—and he did—she would be squirming out of their engagement come midnight when his peril had ended.

The children were hopping, and all around were smiles, except for the two instigators of this plan, Charity Putnam and Sally Fitzhugh.

Perhaps he should bring in MacNab, and the two could propose to him.

Miss Gurnwood was counting something on her fingers. "We have plenty of Sundays to post banns and have the wedding right after Easter." She clapped her hands together. "You can marry the day of the assembly, and we'll celebrate your marriage at the dance. Oh, it will be perfect, and my brother shall officiate." She grabbed Mrs. Smith and hugged her.

The lady had more passion than Alex had estimated.

The Longview girls, as well as most of the other ladies from the surrounding towns, gathered round to congratulate Mrs. Smith on her fine catch. Charity and Sally had good recruiting skills, bringing out so many ladies on such a blistering cold day.

But of course they'd been after his manly self.

And the silk and muslin, though they didn't know that was already out of his hands.

Barty came up to him with a crooked smile. Alex reached for his hand and shook it.

"Will you be part of Mrs. Smith's dowry?" he asked.

"Sir?"

"I've been needing another groom for a long while. Waiting for you to grow into the job, Barty."

The boy beamed from ear to ear, as he himself must be doing.

Mrs. Smith touched Alex's arm, a serious look on her face. "Barty, gather the others. Miss Gurnwood will tell you what needs doing. And behave." The boy stepped away, and she pulled him back. "Wait. You did so very well." She planted a kiss on his forehead and sent him off, red-faced. "Mr. Grant, is there some place where we may talk?"

Talk. She wanted to talk. He grinned and began crafting his battle plan, leading her off to the private dining room.

"Room's not used much," Alex said, piling wood on the fire and dusting off his hands. "Though you've been in here many a time tossing their ladyships' children about."

She nodded. "They've been good to me, very good." She took in a deep breath, and he reached for her hands. "My marrying you will leave them in the lurch."

"Ameline Dawes's marriage to Lord Wallenford didn't." He smoothed his hands over her shoulders. The girl was cold to her bones. And he must rattle those cold bones and go straight to the heart of it, though pain the both of them, it would. "Myra, I don't believe that's your true worry. I believe you're afraid I'll get you with child and you'll die giving birth."

Her chin jerked up, her eyes widened. "Who told you—" She dropped her head and huffed out a breath. "Mrs. McClintock."

"No. MacNab poked around in your past."

Her color rose, and he touched his forehead to hers. "But do not worry. He didn't find more than the story of Artie's birth. Is it true? You stopped breathing?"

"So Lady Wallenford said. She was there." Her eyes shone with tears.

"I couldn't bear to lose you." He touched his lips to hers, but she pushed away.

"Tomorrow, I'll release you from this promise. I've saved you," she said. "Saved your investment. Saved William."

"William?"

"From your father. Auntie Liv said the laird sent MacNab to take the boy."

His brain worked through the words sluggishly, probably because the blue eyes staring up at him were so filled with...feeling.

"I believe Old Grant is plotting to get the boy, but he shall not. He's my son."

"But...he isn't. Auntie Liv told me the truth."

"Did she then?"

The price of the old lady's help was spilling his secrets.

"'Tis my name on the birth record. No one can prove otherwise. He might just as well be mine, come early."

"You would lie?"

"For the sake of a child's welfare? Aye. And so would you."

Her gaze dropped to the twist of his neck cloth and the buttons on his waistcoat.

Guilty, as charged. But how could she admit it and still protect Arthur?

"Will MacNab keep investigating me?" she asked.

"If he does, I shall grab him by his short hairs. We've had too many people meddling in our business, Myra. All that matters to me is whether you are free to marry me. Are you?"

Her breath stuck in her chest, and she nodded.

She heard his long exhale and looked up into eyes as blue as her own. They were kind eyes, and serious, all of his usual merriness gone. In fact, all of his casualness was gone also. As often as not, she'd seen him rumpled and garbed for the heavier work of the inn. Today, his hair was trimmed and combed, and he wore his Sunday best coats.

"Will you hear me out, then?" he asked.

Tears sprang, and she blinked them back. "I should not—"

"Please."

She nodded.

He dropped to one knee, still grasping her hands, and her heart fluttered as if it would take wing.

"Myra Smith, I tell you without teasing or flummery that I find you to be a most admirable woman, a woman of grace and beauty. Will you marry me and make me the happiest of men?"

She could hear her own breath coming in short gasps, the temptation to say yes almost overpowering.

But she must say no. Of course, she must.

"Before you answer, hear the rest of what I have to say. I was an officer with the 42nd Regiment of Foot before I became an exalted innkeeper, and though I survived a number of battles on the Peninsula, I succumbed to a different adversary there."

He bit his lip and frowned.

"I caught the mumps. I was...beyond ill. Of a child's ailment, imagine? No good to commanders, no good to my men. When word came of a crisis at home, it seemed wise for me to go home on half-pay until I'd recovered my strength. On the way, I stopped in Edinburgh and saw a physician."

His gaze searched her face, seeking her trust. She squeezed his hand. "Go on."

"The crisis at home was Wills."

His throat moved in a swallow.

"But what of the visit to the physician, Alexander?"

Color rose in his cheeks. "The fever settled in my...my testes. I'm fully capable of fulfilling my husbandly duties, but...well, there's plenty of powder, but no bullets. I can't father a child, Myra."

She blinked and felt her own face warming, his heat pouring into her. She could have this man's touch, and his kisses, and his passion, and not worry about dying again. They'd have Arthur and William, and...

"But, Alexander, what about your baby girl?"

His mouth firmed, and she saw the truth in his eyes.

His wife had left her childbed, he'd said. She'd had a lover and she'd gone to him, and the man had rejected her, and she'd come back to this man, this good man.

He would not speak ill of his late wife, he'd said, and she would not ask him to. She did not need to know more. She set her palm to his strong jaw. If she married him, they would start their life with two sons and a daughter, and oh how she wished he were whole enough, and she were brave enough to have a babe that was part of them both.

Tears came again, and she couldn't hold them back.

"Oh, doona cry, lass." He stood and pulled her into his chest. "I remember the day you found your way to Longview the summer before Artie was born. I picked you up off the side of the road where you'd fainted and took you to Mrs. Dawes—Lady Wallenford— in that same cottage where you now live. You were but skin and bones. 'Tis no wonder you had a hard time of it birthing the boy." His hand stroked her back. "If by some chance you were to get with child by me, I'd bring in the best midwife in all of England to care for you."

She pushed away from him, heat flooding her cheeks. "*You* found me on the road?"

"Aye. And I could never forget you. I was relieved to see you return to Longview all plumped up and lovely with your healthy babe to take Mrs. Dawes's spot."

"And you want to rescue me again."

"No, Myra. You don't need rescuing. When you returned, 'twas after my own loss, and I thought to leave you be and have done with marriage. But I find I cannot. I want to take you to wife. I want to love you."

She laughed. "And there's the silk and the muslin."

He quirked his mouth and grinned. "Well, that. It's gone to a new owner already."

"You've sold it?"

Her breath caught. He'd tricked her. She was a fool. She hadn't needed to agree to this false engagement.

"I was in no ways certain *you* would rescue *me*. But you shall have a lovely dress out of it for our wedding. Mrs. McClintock promised."

"What?"

"You said the girls are doing well in their gown-making. I gave all the cloth to Mrs. McClintock. The girls will make up gowns in the newest styles, and we'll sell them and share the profits. If the ladies of Upper Upton don't want them, we'll ship them to a modiste in Lewes."

"Alexander Grant. You have all the answers."

"Oh no, love. I don't have the one firm and final answer I need." He pulled her close again. "And need you, I do, Myra Smith."

The touch of his lips sent her heart dancing. She opened her mouth and kissed him back, with every ounce of courage she could muster, and when the brim of her bonnet poked him, he pulled at the ties, tossed the hat away, and raked his fingers through her hair, scattering pins.

A knock at the door made him raise his head. "Go away," he growled.

The door opened, and MacNab poked his head in.

Myra buried her face in Alexander's shoulder until she heard the older man's chuckle.

"So I see it's decided," MacNab said.

"Is it?" Alexander whispered.

She went up on her toes and kissed his cheek. "Yes."

He whooped and spun her around once, and they faced the old man together.

"A strong woman she is. Aye, old Grant won't like it." MacNab grinned.

"Best get back and tell him," Alexander said. "And shut the door on your way out."

On a clear morning in the first week of April, the Marquess of Wallenford, pulling rank on his peers, escorted Myra down the aisle of the village church and handed her over to Alexander.

"Miss Maria Smythe," Alex whispered. "Fancy meeting you here."

The grin she sent him was lopsided, and there was a sheen in her eyes that forecast waterworks.

"Has she come?" he whispered.

She shook her head. "But my old nurse is here."

He squeezed her hands. His Mrs. Smith was really a Smythe, a Surrey lass, who, when her father cast her out despite the tears of her mother, had heard tell of the Longview home and the work done by Lady Hackwell.

"In time," he said.

She nodded. "Today I am determined to be happy."

"And I also."

The front pews were crowded with the marquess, an earl, and a viscount, their ladies and sundry children...and one Scottish laird. He sent his father a grin and laughed at the glare he received in return. He could always count on Old Grant.

Joy bubbled up in Myra as Alex rushed her down the aisle and lifted her into a carriage. He didn't wait to drive away from the crowd of well-wishers before pulling her into a deep kiss that made her toes curl in her new slippers.

"We'll make quick work of this wedding breakfast," he said. "Agreed?"

"Not too quick, for the children's sake." The patronesses and the children had insisted on hosting their wedding breakfast at Longview. The school room had been turned back into a ballroom, so that even the children excluded from the party that night at the assembly rooms could have a chance to dance.

Later, before the wedding breakfast ended, Alex tossed a shawl around his bride and whisked her out through the kitchens.

"Alex, we have guests."

"We'll see them tonight."

"And where are we—"

"Think you we'll have any privacy at the inn? All of our guest rooms are taken, and Wills is likely to burst into our bedchamber at any time."

He led her up the walk to the cottage and through the door.

Inside, a fire burned brightly, and a tray of food had been set out along with a bottle of wine and glasses.

Alex pulled the shawl away and threw it over a chair. "Five weeks, I've waited."

She smiled. "We've waited." Not that they'd had much choice with children always underfoot. She smoothed her hands over his dark coats. "Quite the challenge with a man so braw and handsome."

She untied his neck cloth and began to unwind it, but he stayed her hand. "I've not had the chance yet to say it, Mrs. Grant, but you've made me the happiest of men today." He kissed each of her hands. "And I'm determined to make you the happiest of women."

"I believe you've accomplished that already."

He blinked. And grinned. "No, lass." He traced a finger down her cheek, along her neck, down the side of her breast and up again. "I've only just started."

MacNab found Mrs. McClintock in her small private sitting room conversing with Lady Hackwell. The other patronesses had gone off with a passel of children, returning to the inn, where the room next to his had been turned into a noisy nursery.

He'd be better off bunking here.

"Your girl's just shown out the last of the guests," he said.

Lady Hackwell rose and took herself off also. He glanced at her empty chair.

"By all means, sit, MacNab."

He smiled his gratitude but went to the window instead. It looked out over the garden toward the cottage. The lights had burned down inside.

"Do you suppose we should roust them? He'll have a tap room full of men clamoring for ale tonight."

The lady came up next to him. "He's hired extra help for the evening, and their children are all in hand. Let them be for one night."

He turned a long gaze toward her. "Has anyone ever told you, you're a fine woman, Mrs. McClintock?"

The End

If you enjoyed this story, please consider leaving a review at the retailer of your choice, Goodreads.com, or BookBub.com

Discussion Questions

1. What was your initial reaction to the book?

2. What did you think of the heroine and the hero?

3. What made the setting and time period unique or important? Could the story have taken place in a contemporary setting?

4. Who was your favorite character and why?

5. What do you see as the theme of the story?

6. Do you think this book would make a good film? If so, who would you cast in the roles?

7. What did you like best about the book?

8. What did you think of the book's length? What would you take out, or what would you add?

A Note from the Author

The idea for *A Leap Into Love* came to me as I was writing a blog for the 2016 Leap Year. Which means, this idea had been sitting with my muse since before I wrote *The Marquess and the Midwife*! If you've read that 2016 novella, you'll recognize the Prologue here as a scene from that story.

In 2017, I finally had a chance to get the words to this Leap Day novella onto paper for a February 2018 release. At some point during those months and months of musing, I realized that the unfortunate Miss Smith from *The Marquess and the Midwife* needed her own happily-ever-after, and the story bloomed with her as the heroine of this small-village, sweet romance.

After a Book Club member reached out to me in 2019, I decided to release *A Leap Into Love* in print with a brand new cover and questions to facilitate discussion. Here it is, just in time for the 2020 Leap Day! As an added bonus, I've included the first three chapters of *The Marquess and the Midwife*.

Many thanks go to editor Alicia Dean for catching all the dangling grammar in my original manuscript. And as ever, I'm grateful to my sister, my children and most of all my own hero, my husband Jim.

I love hearing from readers! You can contact and follow me on Facebook, Twitter, and Goodreads, and check out the Pinterest inspiration boards I've created for my books. For excerpts of all my titles, and my weekly blogs, visit my website, AlinaKField.com.

If you'd like to receive special notices about sales and other news, please consider signing up for my newsletter. I promise I won't spam you or sell your email address!

Best regards and happy reading!

Alina K. Field

An Excerpt from

*The Marquess
and the Midwife*

CHAPTER ONE

IN THE GREAT SPRAWL OF London, where would he find her?

Virgil Radcliffe, Marquess of Wallenford, pushed open the coach door himself and swung out on his good leg.

Hackwell House rose before him, all gleaming windows and freshly painted trim. Last year Steven Beauverde, the latest Earl of Hackwell, had uncovered his own brother's killer. Surely he could help discover a woman gone missing in London.

If she were here. If she still lived.

As the coach wobbled around a corner, Ameline Dawes braced her heels and locked each child to her. "Very soon, girls," she said, infusing her voice with loud cheer.

"Move out of the bloody—"

At the curse from outside she covered their small ears and pulled both little heads tight against her.

"And you'll see Thomas and Robby again," she cried, hoping to drown the coachman's shouted rebuke at whoever had cursed him.

It wouldn't do for those words to fly out in an earl's nursery.

Outside, the streets were just as dank and dreary and dirty as she remembered from her confinement here three years before. London in late December was no place for a lady to bring a babe into the world, and no place for a lady—well, a former gentlewoman—to bring the two squirming souls Ameline had tucked on each side of her, her bright, beautiful girls.

She squeezed her eyes and took a deep breath—fatherless they were, but still the lights of her life.

She'd rather have spent Christmas at their cottage in the grounds of the children's home at Longview, where she worked as a teacher and general healer to the children served by Lady Hackwell's charity, and midwife to the local women. Still, the journey had been uneventful, if one could discount twin tantrums, a bout of motion sickness, and assorted disputes over best access to the windows.

She did discount them, as best as her patience would allow. Between the girls' antics and the muddy winter roads, she was fair wrung out. Well, in truth, she was fair wrung out most days, so why should this one be different?

And from the contents of Lord Hackwell's last express, she could plan on a full night ahead and more stuffed-down worry.

She glanced at her twins and couldn't help smiling. She was rightfully proud that she'd been able to provide for them, and grateful for her benefactress. The trials of the journey were small compared to what Lady Hackwell had done for her. And in spite of her impending confinement, Lady Hackwell had promised a celebration of the girls' Christmas birthday.

Because of her confinement, Ameline could be certain any guest list would be limited to the one old army friend of his lordship who Lady Hackwell had said would be visiting. There'd be no chance she'd run into someone from her past life, before she'd become Mrs. Dawes, teacher and midwife.

"I'm hungry." Dee said in the throaty voice that made people mistake her for a boy.

"Me too." Em echoed her larger twin.

"Soon, little ones."

Outside, crowds bunched and mingled at the edge of the traffic, all that humanity crowded together so a woman could barely breathe. London had never been her favorite destination. And London in a dismal December, the days so short one had scarcely five hours of grey daylight, and so abominably moist one could barely feel any warmth and—

"Look." Dee pressed her nose to the window.

Ameline peeled back her dark mood and forced a smile, reminding herself that London was also a place that could be filled with wonders, especially in the week before Christmas. They'd passed shop windows hung with pine boughs and red ribbons, seen girls hawking tied bundles of mistletoe, and outside, here on the edge of the park, was a swarthy street peddler turning the crank on a hand organ while his uniformed monkey danced.

"That is a monkey," Ameline said. "Like the picture in the book at home."

"Mukkey." Dee bounced against the padded leather of Lord Hackwell's traveling chaise, tossing off the rug that had warmed them, sending Em into a howl.

Ameline rescued the blanket from the floor. As her head came up, the chaise turned a corner into a square lined with massive townhouses.

She settled both girls and tucked the warm wool back around them.

"I want to see," Em moaned.

"Go back," Dee said.

Ameline took in a breath. What with tending to Lady Hackwell and assisting her teacher, Mrs. Crawford, with a birth expected to be difficult, there would be little time for looking at shop windows and monkeys. No time actually. "He was a frightfully funny sight, wasn't he?" They'd turned into Berkeley Square where, *please God*, they'd soon find worthier distractions.

Dee squawked and Em started up with her, the way cats did when a fight was underway.

"Look, Dulciana, Emma. We've stopped."

They had indeed. The door opened and a young man in livery set down the coach stairs. A dark patch covered one of his eyes and part of the scar that ran from his forehead to his jaw.

In the three-and-a-half years since Waterloo, England had been filled with displaced and often permanently maimed soldiers, some who'd served under the earl when he'd been mere Major Beauverde. This was another of Lord Hackwell's veterans, the sharp livery making him look as if he'd rejoined his regiment.

The earl and his lady were ones to take in wounded strays, and didn't Ameline know it.

The footman handed her out and the scents of the city rushed into her lungs—coal smoke and damp, and a flavor one didn't want to think too much about. Why Lady Hackwell had chosen to have her baby in London, instead of her country estate, she couldn't fathom.

Dee and Em jostled each other at the coach door, but both pink mouths opened at the sight of the young man's mangled face. He grinned and whisked them up into strong arms. "There now, little misses, we have a few muddy steps to walk, so I'll just carry you, shall I?"

Dee frowned and put a finger into the deep scar.

Ameline pulled out her instrument bag and followed the footman past two noble townhouses, to the gleaming door of Hackwell House. Another coach had blocked the way of their chaise, and servants unloaded baggage from it.

The hair on her neck fluttered. The coach was black with a burgundy trim, large and comfortable...

No. It could not be his. There were many such coaches about. This one, as grimy as it was, might even be hired.

The coach must belong to the friend Lady Hackwell had written about, the army friend who'd returned from roaming the Continent and begged a room with them. He'd be no bother to the ladies, she'd said.

The guest wouldn't be *him*. *He'd* never mentioned Lord Hackwell's name, and besides, *he* had his own grand house in town.

Strange that a man would visit during his hostess's lying in, and stranger still that the Hackwells would allow it. He must be a very good friend, indeed. And perhaps he might keep his lordship distracted during the worst of the labor.

In any case, it was none of Ameline's affair. She was no more than a special kind of servant in this business.

As she drew nearer the visitor's coach, she could see the gold tip of a heraldic shield, the rest of the insignia lurking under a coat of road grime.

Her heart thundered, and inside her gloves, her hands heated and chilled. The crosses and poppies of the Wallenford arms had been burned into her memory, but surely they were not hidden there. And surely, this coach was too tired and beaten up to be that special, grand, and very comfortable coach commissioned by the last marquess.

Tears welled and she blinked them back.

Don't be a ninny. It wasn't him. The last mention of him had been a news item that'd put him in Vienna doing some fusty task for the Crown, a task entirely inappropriate to his character. And good riddance.

And she had her own work to do. Her heart quaked and she took a deep breath to settle it. She'd been in attendance with expert midwives at many births, but this was only the third she would manage, on her own, since Mrs. Crawford was down with her back. And the other new mothers had been farmers' wives.

But...this was London, and if needs must, Lady Hackwell could call on one of Mrs. Crawford's other apprentices as well as the best accoucheur. Ameline could have the coachman return in an hour with fresh horses and be on her way home with the girls.

Yes. That would be better entirely. Her ladyship would be in good hands, and Ameline could dodge this guest of the Hackwells, whoever he might be.

Heart clanging again, she stopped short and lifted her hand to hail her chaise, only to spot it pulling away. Another servant carrying her and the girls' baggage all but plowed into her.

"Mrs. Dawes." A young maid rushed down the steps and tugged Em from the scarred footman's arms.

"Jenny." Squealing, Em crushed herself against the maid, while Dee wriggled in the footman's arms.

Ameline greeted the maid, a Longview girl who'd gone into service, and under the impassive gaze of the starched butler, Alton, they slipped in and handed over their cloaks.

Her breath eased. No handsome noblemen lurked in the hall, only servants, but a staircase loomed, shadowed at the top, daring her to risk the journey to her ladyship's room.

"The pains are started, and her ladyship keeps asking after you," Jenny said. "I'll take these two. Thomas and Robby are waiting for 'em."

Thomas and Robby were Lord Hackwell's young brother and nephew, respectively, both hellions.

Ameline hesitated.

Jenny grinned. "Don't worry. I'll keep the peace in the nursery, and the kitchen maid is there too. Mary's with Lady H."

Mary, Lady Hackwell's longtime maid-of-all-work, now ran the nursery and could easily handle four boisterous children. But her steady hand in the birthing room would be a blessing.

"Don't let them run about. They must stay in the nursery, out of the way of his lordship and his guest."

"Yes, mum, and a great lord is 'e, this guest. 'E's just arrived." Jenny took both girls by the hand. "And ever so 'andsome," she whispered with a cheeky grin. "Now let's go 'ave a biscuit before Master Thomas eats 'em all."

Ameline watched them head up the stairs, swallowing her own smile. She had tried very hard, but there'd always be a touch of the Seven Dials in Jenny.

And perhaps the world was better for that.

A masculine throat cleared. "May I carry your smaller bag, Mrs. Dawes?"

The white haired butler already held her large traveling case in one hand. The scarred footman had disappeared with the children's things. "I'll carry this one," she said. "Lead the way to her ladyship."

"Would you not like to freshen up first?"

She checked the hem of her skirt. She'd mostly kept it out of the mud, but Mrs. Crawford said cleanliness must always be the first medicine applied. She had a fresh work dress in her bag, and it would be good to be able to wash.

"Yes, thank you, and I will be but a moment."

"We are a bit short-staffed, but I can send up a kitchen maid to help—"

"No." She'd long ago abandoned dresses that required a maid. "Best to put her to heating water."

"Very well." He led her up the richly carpeted stairs. "Your chamber is just this way."

An Aubusson runner stretched from one closed door at the far left of the stairs to an opposing one at the other end. As she turned to follow Alton, she heard the click of a door latch and glanced over her shoulder. A man was exiting the far room, his form and face lost in the shadows. She turned quickly and entered her chamber.

*****

Virgil struggled into a clean shirt and coat by himself. He'd left his own man in Dover, waiting for the rest of his crates and dealing with the infernal tedium of customs. In any case, Kimble was a secretary, not a valet. He'd dispensed with those ages ago in Vienna when he caught one out as a spy—for Austria, no less.

And there was little help to be found in the house because Hackwell had sent most of his servants off to have Christmas with their families.

He chuckled. Unconventional, Hackwell was, and his lady too, apparently, though Virgil had not had the pleasure of meeting her, and wasn't likely to, under the circumstances.

The old butler had put him in a room fronting the square, the heavy curtains and thick glazing still leaking in traffic noise, but never mind. He generally drank his way to sleep, anyway.

Murmuring voices were barely audible in the corridor. Hackwell had greeted him at the front door, threatening to send up a repast, and Virgil would have none of it. A night of drinking with his old commander would be just the thing, for both of them, probably. Hackwell had looked none too composed before running off to check on his lady.

Virgil limped to the door and stepped out. At the other end of the corridor, the butler was ushering a guest—a woman—into a chamber.

The skin on Virgil's neck prickled, and when she cast a glance back in profile, his breath caught. Her bonnet obstructed all but a straight nose, full lips, and a determined chin.

She was the right height, the right stature also. Before he could see more, Alton blocked his view, and the door closed on her.

He shook his head. The dress, dark, plain, and ugly, was wrong. His sister's companion had always favored more colorful dresses.

How very odd.

Hackwell's ancient retainer hurried over. "Is there aught that you need, milord?"

"Thank you, I am well settled. I see there is another guest."

The butler inclined his head. "That is the midwife."

"Indeed." He swallowed a smile and went to find the master of the house. Leave it to Hackwell to give the midwife a better room than a marquess.

Annabelle Beauverde, Lady Hackwell, opened the bedchamber door herself and pulled Ameline into as much of a hug as she could manage around her great swollen belly.

"My water has burst," she said, "and the pain is coming at regular intervals. And I am pacing, as you advised me to do."

The pain etched on her ladyship's face drove away all of Ameline's own worries. She had a knack for this, even Mrs. Crawford had said so. Here was a woman who needed her, and here she would be, and stay, until—please, God—the child was safely delivered and the mother in good health.

Lord Hackwell slipped an arm around his wife's shoulder. "Shall I stay? Do you not think she should lie down, Mrs. Dawes? Can all of this walking be good for her?" He ran his free hand through his hair.

His *trembling* free hand.

Ameline glanced around the room. Mary stood nearby wringing her own shaking hands.

Husbands generally made everyone more nervous and got in the way.

Ameline infused her smile with confidence. "Yes, I shall have you lie down now, my lady, so I can examine you. Mary, I will need your help with that. Lord Hackwell, if you could but just have Alton see that the kitchen has started the kettles boiling?"

He tugged his wife to him and kissed her tenderly. Ameline's eyes clouded and she turned away, setting out her instruments, trying to ignore his whispered endearments.

A new mother was blessed to have a man who cared so.

She heard Lady Hackwell's sharp intake of breath and turned to see her clutching her husband's arm.

His jaw tightened and his face paled. "I'm staying, love."

"Mary." Ameline signaled the maid, who hurried over. "My lord, the pain is quite normal. It is merely the body pushing the baby out, and it takes quite a bit of it to accomplish the task. Did not Mrs. Crawford explain? There now, my lady, Mary will help you to the bed, and I'll have a look at this wee one."

When Hackwell stayed frozen, she leaned closer. "Sir."

His gaze tracked the maid leading his wife to the big tester bed.

"My lord." Ameline edged even closer. "Your nerves will make this harder for her," she whispered.

"Ameline is right," Lady Hackwell called, her voice surprisingly strong. "I shall be fine. Don't worry, Steven. Go and chat with Lord Wallenford."

Wallenford. The room around her went as grey as if the fog had been sucked in through the fireplace. Ameline blinked away black spots and clutched the edge of a nearby table, her heart pounding wildly.

When she'd recovered her breath, Lord Hackwell was gone, and two pairs of eyes watched her, startled and round.

Heat rose in her, and she forced her hands to unclench. She must pull herself together. *Her* nerves would make everything harder. Beastly Wallenford didn't matter. Only Lady Hackwell and her babe mattered.

Wallenford was a guest of the Hackwells—a friend of the Hackwells. Oh, yes, he was very good at making friends, very personable, very kind. She must do her job, and then she and her girls would leave, as quickly and quietly as possible.

LADY HACKWELL CLOSED HER EYES AND slumped between Mary and Jenny, face dripping, hair falling loose at her shoulders.

Ameline mopped gently at her patient's face. "You're doing just as you ought," she said, mustering a reassuring tone, though in truth, she was a bit worried. Instead of increasing in frequency, the last few pains had slowed.

"Let's have you stretch out and I'll examine you again." She went to the basin and found the water not just tepid, but murky. *Where is that blasted girl with the water?*

She took a deep breath. "Jenny, what could be keeping the maid? It's been a good thirty minutes since you ran down there."

"One of the girls and the footman is in with the children. It's but one girl, Cook, and Alton, and them's busy getting together a tray their lordships ordered."

Jenny had connived a way to be in the birthing room, and Ameline was glad of it. Apparently though, the kitchen staff gave Lord

Hackwell's needs precedence over Jenny's instructions.

"You go, Ameline," Lady Hackwell wheezed out. "I'll just have a wee rest 'til the next pain, and Mary will help me with a sip of the caudle."

"Ach, I fear it's gone cold also," Mary said. "Do go, Mrs. Dawes. You've not had even five minutes."

"They'll listen to you, Mrs. Dawes," Jenny said.

Lady Hackwell sent her a tired smile.

Fatigue crept over her and she swallowed it down, studying the woman in her care. If the pains continued to slow, she'd send word to Mrs. Crawford. Her bad back notwithstanding, Mrs. Crawford would come, and if need be, she'd secure the best accoucheur in London for Lady Hackwell.

"Go," Lady Hackwell said. "Visit the water closet. Whip Alton into shape. We'll wait right here for you."

She took a deep breath, clearing her head. "Right, then," she said, and hurried out.

"Devil take it, Major—er, Hackwell, can you not sit down?" Virgil poured out the last drops of brandy and handed them to his friend. "That's the end of it."

Hackwell tossed back the drink, and paced to the window. The dark curtains had been pulled closed against the London night. He raked them back to look out. "It's been hours," he muttered. "How long do these things take?"

"Hours and more hours, I hear." Virgil glanced at the empty bottle and the tray littered with dishes. "Come, let's play another hand and I'll beat you again."

He'd deemed it wise to lay out his own topic later, when Hackwell was less distracted. And so, they'd played endless games of *vingt-un* and drunk their way through the open bottle of brandy, discussing the years since they'd last seen each other.

Hackwell grunted but came and plopped down. "This will be you some day, Wallenford. You'll have to marry and go through this."

He smiled and dealt cards. "It's all my mother writes about. 'Come home and marry.' She dearly wants grandchildren."

Hackwell rewarded him with a chuckle. "Worried you'd bring home some Austrian?" He threw out a card.

"An opera singer disguised as a grand duchess."

Hackwell whooped. "By God, I don't envy you marching down the lines at Almack's checking how straight a girl's back is and the size of her decolla—"

"Dowry." He laughed and Hackwell joined him. "There now, you've won this hand, Major. All this talk of matrimony distracted me."

"Well, let me badger you more. What lucky young miss do you have in your sights? Perhaps Bella and I can help, though I must say, we are not considered good *ton*."

He thought of the midwife's profile. He'd spotted *her* in every city he'd visited—only to be disappointed when the girl had been too tall, or too short, or too anything but her.

"Or I suppose you want to look over the season's latest offerings."

"Not at all," Virgil said. "I know exactly the girl I want to marry. I just have to find her."

"Well now, here's a distracting story. I'm all ears."

"Yes, well, I thought perhaps you might be able to help, having sleuthed out your brother's killer."

Hackwell frowned.

"She lived with the family as a companion. After I went up to London to fetch news of Boney's escape, she left."

"Hell and damnation, man. She's the one who sent you that infernal letter that launched you into a three day binge."

He shook his head. "No." At least, not exactly. It had only been her name on the signature line. "She left without a character. My man of business traced her as far as London."

Hackwell tapped the table, pursing his lips. "Pretty?"

"Yes."

"No character, and in London. You realize the odds are good she may have had to make her way—"

"On her back. I know. That alone wouldn't stop me. I owe her."

"You compromised her?"

I loved her.

His heartbeat quickened. At least there'd been no accusation in Hackwell's tone. "Yes. Not my finest hour."

Except, in spite of Dulciana's death, in spite of his mother's intractable sadness, and his brother's bullying, it had been the finest few weeks of his life. Because of her.

"By God, we'll find her. If anyone can find a lost woman in London, it's my Bella."

A muffled cry filtered through the ceiling. Hackwell jumped out of his seat.

"Why not go check on her again, Major?" Hackwell had made three forays into the labor room.

"And have Mrs. Dawes toss me out of my own bedchamber again?" He looked at his empty tumbler. "Blast it, Wallenford, where are all my servants?"

Their last two tugs on the bell pull had gone unanswered. He stood and saluted. "I'll make a sortie to the kitchens for you, Major."

Hackwell stopped short and grinned. "Well, hell, Wallenford. I like the idea of a marquess waiting on me. Break down the door of my butler's pantry if you must, and bring back some bottles."

Virgil grabbed a candle and found his way to the servants' staircase, his bad leg barely paining him. Well, and that was the power of brandy.

Except for an occasional muffled shout, the house was understandably quiet. Hackwell had lost track of the hour, and most of the skeleton staff should be abed. Those who were not were most likely engaged with helping in the birthing chamber. Even he, a bachelor, could work that out.

One floor above the kitchens, he heard voices and saw a light.

"There now, 't'will be soon, Alton, and all will be well."

Virgil's foot paused above the stair and he gripped the banister. The woman's soothing tones had reached up to warm him in a familiar way.

"Have more brought up as soon as possible."

She was ascending the stairs toward him.

He blew out his candle and stepped down.

Ye gods, but her ladyship needed more maids, and a couple more footmen with both arms and both legs, at least for this type of fetching and carrying.

Ameline chided herself for being insensitive and balanced the steaming bucket. She set down the lamp momentarily to gather her skirts, along with the lamp handle.

A pair of men's boots moved into view and the lamp bobbled. Fine boots they were.

She sighed, gritting her teeth. Lord Hackwell's visits had unnerved his lady, and Ameline had counseled him to leave.

Very well, she'd thrown him out, once almost literally. He would wonder what *she* was doing below stairs. He might send for the accoucheur he was mumbling about, and his lady would not like it.

"I've just popped down to the kitchen for a word with Alton, my lord," she said. "All is going well, except he's a bit short on staff."

"We have noticed that."

The skin on her back rippled and she shivered. This wasn't Hackwell—it was *him.*

Panic flared in her and her hands and ankles began to tingle. He carried no light. She let her own lantern dip lower and stepped to one side. What was he doing on the servants' staircase in the middle of the night?

If he saw her, he *would* remember her, but he would not *want* to, unless he would think to *befriend* her again. Heat flamed in her.

She took in a breath. "Let me pass, *Lord Hackwell,*" she said.

"Let me carry that bucket for you."

"No." She forced in another breath, willing herself to speak calmly. "That is, no thank you. I shall send a servant for you when it is time."

Footsteps scurried on the stairs. "Mrs. Dawes?" Jenny called, breathless.

Her heart raced again. She'd tarried too long in the kitchen. "I'll be right—"

Heat touched her hand as the bucket came out. The lantern, too, lifted higher, and she looked up into the face of Lord Virgil Radcliffe, now the latest Lord Wallenford.

"*Mrs. Dawes?*" His eyes widened and then narrowed, and his lips curved down.

Anger spiked in her. "*Lord Wallenford.*"

He moved down to the step below her, putting them at eye level, and crowded her against the hand rail.

"Give me the bucket, sir. I can manage quite well without your help." Quite, quite well.

"Can you, indeed?" he drawled, sounding just like his brother the day he'd sacked her.

Blast him. Blast the Wallenfords. Blast the Hackwells. "Alton has a bottle set out. Best go and fetch it."

His lips quirked.

She gritted her teeth. "Give me the blasted bucket, Virgil."

"Mrs. Dawes?" Jenny stepped closer and reached for the bucket handle. "Begging your pardon, but she must hurry, my lord."

Virgil's gaze turned on the saucy maid, and Ameline silently saluted her. Jenny had survived as a child in the rookeries—no mere marquess would frighten her.

"Very well," he said. "Carry the bucket for the *lady.*"

Her hand fisted around the lantern handle and she saw the candle he fumbled with, still dripping wet wax.

He'd deliberately snuffed it out. He'd known it was her. He'd known about her. And how?

"We'll talk later, Mrs. Dawes."

A loud moan snaked its way down the stairs from the upper floors, driving out all thoughts of Wallenford.

"Eat, Hackwell." Virgil began filling a plate from the dishes he'd helped Alton carry up from the kitchen. "You must eat, else you'll be bowsy when you greet your heir."

Hackwell grunted and took a bite. "Did you wake Cook, Wallenford? Don't tell me you and Alton pulled all these dishes together yourself."

Virgil forced a laugh. "You'd be surprised. I believe all of your servants are in the kitchen boiling water for Mrs. Dawes." He poured himself a brandy. "Who, by the way, I met on the staircase, on her way up from dressing down the staff for not being quick enough to answer her demands."

Hackwell lifted an eyebrow.

Finally, he'd managed to distract Hackwell, and not by what he'd said. The man was too perceptive by half.

"A memorable encounter, I take it?"

A memorable encounter that stirred other memories. The dim light of the lantern had only enhanced her full lips and dark, intense eyes. And the more he thought about it, she'd filled out, too, from the underfed waif to a woman with more generous curves under her serviceable gown.

"Pour me some of that." Hackwell slid over his glass. "A fetching young woman, is she not? She's the midwife, as you've probably deduced. We could have brought in one of these fashionable man-midwives, but I'm not fond of another man fiddling about in my wife's privates, and as Bella said, one wonders how someone who's not been through the experience can be totally effective. And anyway, Mrs. Dawes is one of my wife's bluestocking friends. I quite like her."

The rambling words clanged about in Virgil's brain. Ameline, a bluestocking, a midwife, and friend to a countess.

And married. Perhaps she'd just adopted that term of address in the course of her duties.

She couldn't be married. It wasn't possible, was it? Not without a dowry, and Ameline had never had one, had she? But of course there could be other men besides him who'd take her without a dowry. Mr. Dawes must care for her.

Like *he* cared for her. And she was supposed to be *his*. "Where is Mr. Dawes while his wife is running about birthing babies?"

Hackwell scratched the dark stubble on his chin. He'd loosened his neck cloth and coats, the expectant father all at his leisure. "Dead. Bella said she's a widow."

His body heated and thrummed. Dead.

"If you can't find your missing woman, are you interested? She's gentry stock, I believe, but in the conventional order of things, beneath a marquess."

Heat spiked in him and his lungs filled again. Dead, dead, the husband was dead. Ameline was widowed, his missing woman. He could have her beneath him again.

He'd never been one for whores and actresses, and even after his injuries had healed, he'd not had a woman since Ameline—no one had appealed.

But *she'd* found someone. *She'd* married.

Through the tangle of thoughts, another muffled sound reached them, and then a cry, like a cat mewling.

Hackwell shot out of his seat, tightening his neck cloth, and began pacing.

The knot was crooked and the uneven sides of his waistcoat flapped about. "You might want to shave before you greet your lady wife," Virgil said. "Or at least button that coat properly."

Hackwell waved a hand. "For the love of God, distract me, Wallenford. It's the only reason I'm allowing you to stay here during this infernal ordeal. Yes, I'll help you find your woman, but why are you in London in my townhouse instead of your own?"

He groaned. He'd been airing his troubles with solicitors and money lenders. He'd hoped to avoid discussing them with peers. But Hackwell had been his commander during his brief military career, and then his friend while they were both in Vienna. He could be trusted. "The usual reasons."

Hackwell inclined his head to the door and began fumbling buttons. "Estate in disarray?"

The man had an uncanny ability to hold more than one target in his sights. "Yes. My father and brother didn't manage as well as I'd thought."

"Been through the same thing. You shall have my help—mine, my wife's and my steward's, if you want it."

"Good of you, Hackwell."

"Yes, well, good that you came back. It's hard to manage finding a woman and fixing an estate from the Continent. And as you say, your mother has been hounding you to return."

"Yes." His mother and others. The last letter had come from his brother's former betrothed, Caroline Jermyn, urging him to return for his mother's sake. That letter had done the trick, though not for the reasons Caroline had put forward. "I've stayed away as long as I could. Now I'm rearranging debts and pursuing some other avenues." Footsteps shuffled in the corridor, the sound growing louder. "We have minerals to exploit, and we're in dire need of some new agricultural practices."

Hackwell nodded as he moved to the door, opening it before the messenger could knock.

A maid, an older one than the girl he'd seen on the stairs, bobbed a curtsy. "It's a girl, milord. And Mrs. Dawes, she says to tell you she's a healthy mite, and that her ladyship is well, and she will send for you as soon as her ladyship and the room are cleaned up and put right."

Hackwell whooped and clamped hands on the maid's shoulders, just short of a hug. The shocked woman gave him a lopsided grin and ran off.

Virgil filled their two glasses again and met Hackwell halfway, raising a toast. "To your new daughter. Have you come up with a name?"

"Little Lady some-such, devil take it. I shall let Bella name her." He smiled broadly. "A girl."

"Disappointed it's not a boy?"

"Hell, no, man. You're not one of those jackanapes clamoring for an heir to safeguard the entail, are you, Wallenford?"

"No. My mother is doing all of the clamoring. Ends every letter with a reminder."

"Does your missing woman have money? She could solve two problems."

He groaned. "Not you, too."

Hackwell laughed. "Bella's money saved the tenants' roofs, but even without it I'd have married her and got out my ladder and hammer. And she can give me ten girls and I'll be happy. I had no mother or sisters or even girl cousins growing up, and now I'm raising my nephew and brother. You at least had your mother to bring a feminine presence into your life."

"I had a sister, also."

"Devil take it. I didn't know that."

"She was...never quite up to the family standards. Kept her hidden away in the country. Dulciana died a few months before my brother."

Hackwell's head shot up. "Dulciana?"

"That was her name."

"An unusual name." Hackwell's eyes narrowed.

Virgil's neck itched, and an ache started around his heart. Dulciana had been the family's dark secret, the imperfect child stowed away in the nursery. His twin, damaged at birth. He was never supposed to talk of her. "I suppose so."

A tap at the door brought news that her ladyship was ready to receive her husband's visit.

Hackwell waved a hand at the still loaded trays. "I'll leave that feast to you, Wallenford."

Virgil took the bottle and a glass and retired to a dark corner, prepared to drink his way through the rest of the night. The mention of his sister, and the appearance of Ameline, a widowed Ameline, set his spirits dancing between melancholy and anger and, truth to tell, hope.

He'd expected to have to look harder for her. He'd expected to find her at some godforsaken manor, wrangling brats, or wiping an old lady's arse. Or worse, flat on her back in one of the houses in St. James's.

He'd not seen her since his brother, the last marquess, sent him off to London to find out about Bonaparte's escape from Elba.

To get him out of the way. After he left, Ameline had packed her bags and departed without giving a reason. So Virgil had been told.

He'd written to his mother for news, and enlisted Baker, the family's harried steward and Virgil's childhood friend, to find Ameline while he went off to Belgium with Wellington's crew. And then, Ameline's letter had arrived, enclosed in one from his brother, telling him not just goodbye, but good riddance.

It had taken him three wasted years to know who had written that goodbye, years of running away, years of Ameline finding and perhaps loving another man, a man who was not Virgil. The thought raised an ache in all his mangled parts.

He lifted his glass and paused. Perhaps there was a better fix tonight than getting himself foxed. She was free now, and so was he.

The study door opened and a figure slipped in.

Virgil bobbled his glass, sloshing brandy onto the table, and setting it down quietly.

A MELINE HURRIED TO THE LADEN table, pulled off her cap, and massaged her temples. As births went, this one had been blessedly routine. A child came on God's time, and the journey exhausted the mother and the midwife, the mother's labor wrenching Ameline's insides as if she were experiencing childbirth again herself.

She pulled over a plate and filled it, grateful to take this bone-weary repast alone in the quiet of Hackwell's study. A branch of candles illuminated the table, but outside the circle of light all was shadowed. The smell of leather bound books, tobacco, and the low fire reached her, bringing back memories of home, and the room where her father secluded himself when he needed solitude.

Her fork clacked on the plate, her knife sawing ineffectually, until she abandoned politeness and picked up a piece of ham in her fingers, taking a large bite and chewing. "Mmm, that's good," she mumbled around a mouthful, a chuckle rising within her. She could never be so improper around the children. *A lady is a lady, even in private.* She'd used her mother's gentle rebuke on her own girls, as well as the girls at the children's home.

She squeezed her eyes shut. She'd not been a lady in private with Virgil Radcliffe. In fact, that lapse had sealed her future. If not for the kindness of others, and if not for Mr. Dawes...well, gentry or no, she was no longer a lady, and in this quiet moment didn't have to put on high and mighty manners for Dulciana and Emily's sake.

A flash of movement in the corner sent the hair on her neck dancing and her ham clattering against the utensils.

Oh God, no.

A shadow rose, took form and approached the table. She wiped her hands and reached for her cap.

"Leave it, Ameline."

Virgil's rich baritone sent chills down her spine. He'd always claimed to love her mousy brown hair, seeing hints of gold that no one else could.

Hands shaking, she pulled the cap over her head ungracefully, shoving loose locks under. "Go to the study, he said," she croaked. "Have something to eat, he said." Suspicion threaded through her, but she quickly pushed it away. Hackwell had been muddle-headed, not manipulative, sending her here. "I shall leave you in peace, *Lord* Wallenford."

She tried to push back her chair, but his hand clamped down on the back of it.

Her pulse quickened. If she but leaned back, the hard knots of his knuckles might ease the tight fibers around her spine.

And the thought made her face heat. Virgil's power over her hadn't abated. He could still reduce her to a besotted fool.

No. She squeezed her eyes shut and remembered her own hours and hours of wrenching labor birthing twins. She was strong. She could master this. She would not be left alone again in a puddle of foolish sensibility.

"Stay. Finish eating. *Mrs.* Dawes."

She opened her eyes and let out a breath. A hint of anger had colored Virgil's tone, and her nerves prickled. He'd never been like his father or his brother. He wouldn't have raised a hand to a woman before. What sort of man was he now?

Mrs. Dawes. It was the *Mrs.* that had his voice breaking. Her marriage upset him. While he traipsed about the world, he thought she would have waited, penniless and friendless, raising his children.

Her thoughts flew to the nursery, where the girls would be rising soon. She clutched the edge of the table. How much had Virgil learned about her and her girls from Hackwell?

Seconds ticked by. Finally, he released her chair, pulling another over and seating himself next to her, propped himself on an elbow, his green gaze making her skin prickle.

She turned what she intended to be a defiant look upon him, and her stomach fluttered. On the stairway, she hadn't had enough time or light for a good look. The years of battle, and serving the Crown, and inheriting a title and all that great responsibility had carved lines into Virgil's face and made him even more impossibly handsome. His dark hair curled and tangled, his beard sprouted in a dark scruff, and his green eyes flashed darkly in the candlelight. Blackbeard, his sister Dulciana used to call him with a giggle, raking her fingernails over his jaw.

As Ameline had also done.

The knot in her stomach moved up to her throat. *I want you still. Even though you deserted me.* She grabbed a glass of dark liquid, swallowed and choked as it burned through her.

She took in a deep breath. "The Marquess of Wallenford."

"Mrs. Dawes, midwife. He leaned close. "A squire's daughter, working as a midwife."

"Yes, indeed. I'm quite good at it, and I like it."

He flinched, and she realized, he did not like being the marquess, and that was not surprising. Virgil had always had more capacity for fun and adventure than the two dour men who'd preceded him in the title. His traveling the last three years must have fitted him better, even if the duties hadn't.

What if he hadn't gone off? What if his brother hadn't died? What if they'd found a way together?

She tried to shrug off those thoughts, but he pursed his lips, and warmth shot through her center. He'd kissed her with those lips, everywhere.

"You're very lucky then," he said.

Lucky? How was she lucky? She, a gentleman's daughter, had struggled through birthing twins. Bastards. This man's girls.

Tears threatened, and she blinked them back. She had beautiful girls, and perhaps he was right. She'd been blessed beyond belief to find women who'd helped her. There'd been a trace of envy in his voice, and why? He'd inherited a title, and he'd fallen in with Hackwell as a friend, and Hackwell was known to be a decent sort.

"And you're a marquess. Shall I offer condolences or congratulations? Perhaps both." She pushed the plate back. "And now, I shall leave you in peace."

He dragged the plate close and picked up her utensils. "Stay, Ameline. Talk to me." He sawed at the meat, carving it into small pieces. "These are very good nibbles, as you used to say to my sister. And you're very hungry."

She swallowed a lump. She was. Or, she had been. He stabbed a morsel of meat and lifted it to her. "Take a bite."

The air around her quaked with the scent of the meat and the essence of Virgil, a scent that defied conscious awareness. She accepted the bite and slid it from the tines of the fork, chewing slowly, her heart beating a fierce tattoo, her belly rumbling with carnal hunger that rested somewhat lower than her stomach.

"When did you last eat?" he asked, bringing her attention higher.

The meat clogged her throat, and she choked again.

He handed her a cup of tea. "Drink this. Though I'm afraid it's gone cold."

I haven't.

Another piece of meat stood ready in his steady hand for transport into her trembling mouth.

"Your last meal, Ameline?" he asked, sternly.

"This morning." She said.

"What? You had no meal before leaving your, er, lodgings, to come here?"

His gaze fixed on her. He was fishing—he thought she lived in London.

Her mind jumped ahead and sent her heart plummeting. Hackwell would tell him where she lived, and if he wished to bother her, he jolly well would ride out to Sussex and do so.

The meat she'd just swallowed formed a lump in her chest. And what of her girls? He was a marquess. No matter how she declared Mr. Dawes their father, one could look at them and know they were Virgil's. And once he met them, once he saw them, he *would* try to take them.

She waved his fork away. "I reside in the country."

"Please eat, Ameline." His touch on her arm sent shivers through her.

She pulled away. This could not be. "I've lost my appetite." Such a liar, she was. "If I'd known you would be here, I'd have insisted Lady Hackwell call in someone else to attend her."

"Why?"

"I have no wish to see you, ever again." That was only a half-lie. She wished to do more than see him—she wished to thrash him for what he'd done to her, for the way he'd promised to help and then left.

"Tell me of your husband."

When she looked, Virgil's face had gone tight, his jaw locked, and what she saw calmed her. He was not so at ease this night either.

"My husband...is no more." That was less of a lie than saying he was dead.

"You're a widow?"

She nodded. "And now, I will leave." She pushed back her chair and stood.

His hand shot out and took hers, sending electricity up her arm, like the lightening striking Mr. Franklin's kite.

"I don't care about your title, Wallenford. I won't be bullied." *Or seduced. Dear God.*

"Is that what I'm doing?" A grin spread across his face, Virgil's grin, playful and free, and for a moment she was back in his sister's set of nursery rooms watching him tease Dulciana.

He stroked his thumb over the back of her hand. "Oh, I suppose I am. And what good is a title if you can't bully people, Ameline. That was always Father's rule."

He stood, keeping hold of her hand. "We were friends once, Ameline. Equals."

Equals? A marquess's younger brother and a hired companion? Well, perhaps they had been equally bullied. He was sent off to war, and she was just sent off. They'd both landed on their feet, but in very different worlds. "You were always Lord Virgil to me."

"You were to take care of Granny after Dulciana died. Why did you leave, Ameline?" His gaze pinned her again.

Her chest ached. He didn't know what had happened. Or, he did and this was some sort of test.

The sort of test she refused to take part in. "It does not matter." She tugged at her hand and his grip tightened. "I had a new opportunity. Let me go, Wallenford." His frown deepened but his grip relaxed and she pulled her hand away. "Now, I really must leave."

She kept to a normal pace, but as soon as the door closed on her she ran up the stairs to her room.

Virgil watched Ameline's departure, gripping the chair like an anchor to keep from following her. He would get her to talk to him, but not tonight. She was shocked, tired, and probably still famished.

Now that he'd found her, he'd need time to woo her. How long would a visiting midwife stay? At least overnight.

He poured a drink, looked at it, and set it down. He could bribe a servant to tell him if she left. In any case, she would stay at least one more day to look after her patient, and probably longer.

And blast it, his other infernal business would keep him tied up tomorrow and the next day.

His mind too filled with plotting to sit quietly and drink, he blew out the candles and headed up to his chamber, so close to hers. If she ran, would it be back to her own home? Tomorrow, he'd work in a few moments alone with Hackwell and find out just where in the country he'd found Ameline Dawes.

Also by Alina K. Field

Rosalyn's Ring
2013

Bella's Band
2014, Soul Mate Publishing

Liliana's Letter
2015, Havenlock Press

The Marquess and the Midwife
A Christmas Novella
2016, Havenlock Press

The Ghost of Depford Hall
A Halloween short story, a sequel
to
Liliana's Letter
2017, Havenlock Press

Haunting Miss Fenwick
2019, Havenlock Press

The Duke She Despised
In the *Winter Wishes Regency Holiday Anthology*
2019

Sons of the Spy Lord Series

Marrying Mr. Gibson
Previously titled *The Bastard's Iberian Bride*
Book One
2017, Havenlock Press

The Viscount's Seduction
Book Two
2017, Havenlock Press

The Rogue's Last Scandal
Book Three
2017, Havenlock Press

The Counterfeit Lady
Book Four
2018, Havenlock Press

Avenging the Earl's Lady
Book Five
2019, Havenlock Press